DISTANT TIMES

by Gary J. Martin

for all of us who made it through

those crazy times and those who did

not.

Amber

He resents me, but it's not my fault. He says that he loves me regardless, but I don't know if that's true. I've tried to believe it, but it gets harder year by year. I'm not sure I can go on like this much longer. Something has to change. Between the stress in our marriage and the pressure that comes with my job as an ICU nurse, I'm about to crack.

I head out after another grueling shift, worrying at every curve as I drive. I pull into the driveway and shut off the engine, but my mind continues to run rampant as I walk to the front door of our home—a home built on honesty and communication that slowly cracked at the foundation.

I pause before I stick in the key. I try to whisk away the anxiety with a deep breath, and then, before I fully realize it, I'm inside. Shane is lying on the couch asleep with an almost empty bowl of what looks like leftover spaghetti on his lap. I decide to let him be. I start to sneak off to take a shower as I do every night, but he must have heard me because he moves, and the bowl of spaghetti falls to the floor. It startles me but not him. He wakes up slowly and picks up the bowl like it's no big deal. It isn't. There is barely any mess.

"Amber?" he says groggily.

"Hey," I say, feeling the effects of fatigue myself.

"How was work?" he says, his eyes almost fully open now.

I sigh. "Horrible."

He doesn't say anything else. He gets up, takes the bowl to the kitchen, then comes back with a rag and proceeds to pick up the noodles with it.

"How was—" I begin to ask him how his day was as I always do, but I already know the answer, and this time the words don't come out. I'm shocked by what does come out of my mouth instead.

"Do you still love me, Shane?"

"What?"

He is floored. If he wasn't fully awake before, he is now. We've had intense conversations about our relationship and the one thing it all boils down to, but I've never come right out and asked him. He chokes out his answer.

"Of-of course I do."

"Shane, please be honest with me. You barely ever touch me anymore. When was the last time we had sex?"

"I-I don't know. I'm sorry."

"I can't do this anymore," I say softly, not wanting to hurt him.

"Do what?"

"I can't have kids, and you've stopped loving me because of it."

"I still—"

"It's OK, Shane. I don't hate you. You don't have to keep pretending. I want you to be happy. I thought our love was stronger, but it's OK. I want you to have a family."

"What are you saying?"

"I'm . . . I'm saying I think we should get a divorce."

"Amber, please. We can work this out. We can go back to the doctor; maybe they can do something else. It's not too late."

"We've tried everything. I'm thirty-eight. It's done. I'm not meant to have a kid, but you still can. You can find someone younger and fertile, and you'll fall in love with her, and you can have your family. It's OK," I say, trying not to cry.

"I-I don't know if I can let you go," he says as tears fill his eyes.

"You can. You have to. I can't go on like this, knowing I can't give you the one thing you've always wanted."

"Amber, I . . . I—"

"Let go, Shane. Just let go."

"You're . . . you're right. I'm sorry. I haven't been fair to you. I know it's not your fault. You deserve someone who will love all of you, no matter what. Are you . . . are you sure? I—"

"I'm sure," I sniffle.

It was a long time coming. The first two years of our marriage we weren't worried about kids. In fact, we proactively made sure we didn't have any. Then we stopped prevention. If it happened, it happened. We both knew we were ready if it did. It wasn't until five years in, me hitting thirty-three, knowing time was running out, that we actively started trying. Then the trying didn't take. I suggested several times that we adopt, but he wants a biological child, someone to pass on his family genes to. I can't blame him for that. Now he will have another chance. A chance with someone else.

It's the hardest thing I've ever done in my life. I should feel relieved that it will soon be over, but somehow, I feel like the worst is yet to come. Something beyond my marriage. I don't know why I feel this way, but it's like a battle against an invisible enemy is on the horizon.

Michael

I'm not like most junior high kids. I
want to go to school. It's not that I like
taking tests and having to read boring
textbooks. It's just that I'm safe there. It's
my only escape. Most of my classmates look
at the clock and count down the minutes
until the final bell. Freedom awaits them.
For me, it's back to prison—back to hell.

I want to run away, but I don't know
where I would go. I don't have any friends.
Even if I did, their parents would just send
me right back home, never knowing what
happens here. I've thought about telling a

teacher what happens, but I don't want them to think anything is wrong with me. What *is* wrong with me? I don't think I did anything bad to deserve it, but I don't know. I keep thinking that it must be my fault. Maybe somehow it is.

Every day right after school, Mother makes me watch the religious channel with her before Father gets in from the field. I couldn't pay attention even if I wanted to, which I don't, because I can't stop thinking about what's coming.

"You need to read your Bible every day, Michael. Each time you step outside this house, you are going into a battle zone. There's all kinds of evil out there."

Not as bad as the evil in this house, I
want to say. She keeps harping at me until
they start singing songs, then she finally
leaves me alone as she sings along. When
the program ends, she switches on the six
o'clock news. Father will be in any moment.

**Breaking news tonight: The
United States has recorded its first
coronavirus death as cases continue to
rise in China and Italy.**

"It's just a matter of time," Mom
says.

"Before what?" I manage to say.

"We're in the last days, Michael. If this virus keeps spreading and it starts killing a lot of people here, too, like it's doing in China, that could be the sign. We have to be prepared."

I try not to let her see that I don't care, but she's too focused on the TV. She barely pays attention to me. She never does. Only when she tries talking to me about God, like right now, which is making me want to shout five million things at her that I know I can't. She's so oblivious to the world, lost in her religion. Her blind faith in Jesus has blinded her to reality, and that's part of the problem. Maybe it's not my fault. Maybe it's her fault. Maybe it's all of our faults. Why is this happening? I don't want to be me. I—

"Did you repent today?" Mother asks, bringing me out of my head for a split second.

"Yes, Mother," I lie.

I'm pretty sure that's not how it works. Once you accept Jesus, it doesn't matter. He forgives you of all your sins, past and present. How does she not know that? She should know more than most. I think it's all a bunch of bullshit. When you're dead, you're dead. That's it. Lights out.

Father comes walking through the door. I turn away and stare at the TV. More news about the virus. A thought pops into my head. Maybe this virus will keep

spreading and kill us all. If God does

somehow exist, then he will spread this virus

as quickly as possible.

Chase

I can't believe it. It's finally going to happen. I'm going to WrestleMania. It's a dream come true. I've been a pro wrestling fan since I was a small child. I still watch it religiously every Monday night, as well as Wednesdays and Fridays. It's the perfect combo of live theater, athleticism, comedy, and drama. In just a few short weeks, I'll be checking wrestling's biggest show off my bucket list.

My best friend, Brad, and I have been killing it the past couple of years with our prestigious lists. Why wait? Last time I checked, we are not guaranteed a certain amount of time on this Earth. Our minds are made up. We are going. I don't have a wife or a girlfriend I need to get approval from, so that helps. No kids either. I've been single all my life. Forty years and counting. Sure, I've had plenty of casual relationships over the years and a few actual girlfriends, but nothing that has gotten to the level of "I love you."

Someday I'd like to say, "I love you" to someone other than my family and friends, but it just hasn't happened for me. As much as I like my freedom, I do get lonely sometimes. After forty years of

16

existence in this consciousness, I'm sure all the good ones are taken.

"Sounds good. Love ya, bro. See ya tomorrow," I say, hugging Brad. That's how we ended our conversation that night at the bar after we had discussed our WrestleMania plans. What he said in the middle of the evening I was not expecting, though.

We were discussing tickets for the event itself; we had already secured our plane tickets. Under one hundred dollars apiece for a round trip was a steal. Granted, we will have to layer up on clothes and only bring small backpacks that fit under our seats so we don't have to pay the outrageous fees of checking bags or buying storage spots in the above bins. It's worth it. It's way better than our original plan of driving nine hours from Charlotte to Tampa, though my buddy and I could have done it easily. We are used to long drives. We've made the twelve-hour drive home to see our families in Cape Girardeau, Missouri, many times since moving to North Carolina on a whim five years ago.

Brad and I lived together for the first year, but we both found decent jobs and got our own places after that. Our jobs don't make us rich, though, so saving money is a priority. I work at a marketing firm, and he is a manager at a grocery store.

"Dude, I think we should hold off on the tickets," he says.

"What? Why?" I ask, clueless and annoyed. He always likes to wait till the last minute to buy tickets to any event we ever go to. Usually, we end up paying more or have to settle for a worse view. This time he made a good point, though it would take me a while to figure it out.

"Prices might drop."

"It's WrestleMania. It's going to sell out. Why would they drop?" I ask, befuddled.

"People might be afraid to go."

"Why would they be afraid to go? I'm sure security for something like this is crazy good."

"No, no. Not because of that. Because of the coronavirus."

"The what?" I say in total confusion.

"The damn coronavirus. You seriously haven't heard of it?"

"No. I don't watch the news. You know that. What the hell is a coronavirus?"

"Some virus from China. The President has already banned people from there from coming into the US because of it," Brad said, picking up his beer.

"Oh, wow, it's that bad?"

"Could be," he says right before taking a drink.

"What does it do to you?"

"It's kind of like a really horrible version of the flu or a cold."

"Damn. Should we not go?" I am very concerned now. I'm a bit of a hypochondriac and, some would say, a germaphobe. Me, I just call it being smart. Wash your hands; don't touch your face. Common sense stuff. But I'll admit I do worry about getting sick and dying. That's why I don't watch the news. I don't need to be reminded of death every day.

"We'll be fine, man. We might be able to score some lower-level tickets for cheap, maybe even ringside," he says.

"That would be pretty sweet," I say, trying to focus on the fun and not the virus. I think about it for a few seconds longer and let my worries wane. I think about sitting in the first row along the ramp and reaching out my hand to touch John Cena's as he walks by. I think about the lights going out and the bell tolling as the Undertaker walks to the ring. The thought of being able to sit close for such an amazing event begins to trump my fear of contracting some disease I just now heard of and know nothing about.

As a whole, we had no clue what was coming.

Chase

I've been watching ticket prices for a week. They don't seem to be going up or down. I've also been—believe it or not—watching the news to learn a little more about this coronavirus.

I'm chillin' on my couch, flipping through the channels, couple minutes' worth of CNN, then two more on Fox News, and I've had about all the news I can take. I click over to ESPN. SportsCenter is on. I'm much more likely to watch that show for longer than two minutes than any other show besides wrestling. A good twenty minutes go by, and I start to fiddle on my phone, looking at fantasy baseball projections after SportsCenter mentions this year's sleeper picks. I begin to text friends to see when they want to have our draft. I look back up at the TV when I hear the words "breaking news," and the dominoes start to fall.

"This astounding and unprecedented story continues to evolve. The NBA is suspending the season."

Immediately, I pick up the phone to call Brad.

"Dude, what the fuck is going on? Are you watching ESPN?" I say, shaking my head over and over.

"Yeah, I just saw. I bet every other sport is going to do the same."

"They can't, man. This is just crazy!" I say, staring at the headline on the TV like it's not real.

"Guess we're just gonna have to go on YouTube and watch all the old classic games for a while," Brad says casually.

"It can't last. Why would the other sports not play if no one is infected? Once they figure out if anyone has the virus, they can isolate those players and make sure all the players and staff are healthy, then start playing again. It can't last *that* long," I say optimistically.

"This shit is spreading like wildfire. I'm telling you, just wait. The other sports are gonna shut down, too. I hope I'm wrong, but I doubt it."

Brad isn't wrong. Over the next few days, the NHL follows suit, suspending its season, and then the worst news of all— MLB delays the start of theirs. It hits me like a ton of bricks. What am I going to do without sports? They are my life. I care about people and want them to be healthy, but this has never happened, ever, I don't think. I just don't know.

The next week I watch more news than I have in my entire life, and though it's still hard for me to believe there's no basketball, baseball, or hockey right now, at least there is still wrestling. Thank God. When I'm watching, it is about the only time I'm not thinking about catching this virus. That is now firmly planted at the forefront of my mind. The news is making it out to be the worst thing that has ever happened in history, and I'm starting to believe it. I've left my house only to go to work and to get food. That's it. Brad keeps wanting to hang out, but I keep telling him no. And now I need to call him again to tell him no to something else.

"I don't wanna go to WrestleMania. It's not worth it, man. I'm sorry," I say. "I wanna go, I really do, but you know how close together the seats are on the plane and in stadiums, and people are going to be yelling and screaming all over each other. I don't wanna get sick, man. What if we get there and start feeling bad, then we get home and wind up in the hospital? Or what if—*just what if*—one or both of us end up dead just because we decided to go to a wrestling show? I can't, man. I can't do it."

"It's OK. I get it, bro. Not going to have to worry about it anyway. There's no way they can have it. Eighty plus thousand people from all across the world. No chance. Hell, they are starting to restrict flights from other places besides China now, too."

"I saw that. Crazy. They can't cancel WrestleMania, though. There's no way," I say, totally believing it is still going to happen, despite every other sport shutting down. I guess that's just how much I love it.

"I bet they do," he says.

Turns out I am right in the end, technically. The WWE decides to move WrestleMania to their performance center in Orlando and hold it in front of no fans. I'm sure that decision was not an easy one to make. I also have some major decisions to make myself. I don't feel comfortable going into the office anymore. I need to get ahead of the curve. There are going to be other curves to worry about soon, as well, and

how to flatten them.

Michael

It's spreading but not quick enough.
Why hasn't one of us gotten sick yet? Day
after day, I watch the news with Mother,
fearing what is to come. Her fear comes
from the TV, but mine comes from what
will happen next. Night after night, she lifts
her hands to the sky and prays over the
world, unaware of what is going on right in
her own home. Soon the news will be over,
and she will go read the Bible while she
takes a bath. I'll be left alone with Father.
He will quietly come to get me, threatening
me with his eyes if I'm still in the living

room and not my bedroom when she shuts the bathroom door. He will wait until he hears the water stop running before it begins.

———

Wednesday nights are the worst. Mother goes to Bible study, and I'm stuck home with Father for a couple of hours. "Can I go with you to church tonight, Mom?" I ask, already knowing what will happen. I hate church, but I hate him way more. I wish I knew the combination to the gun safe. Then I wouldn't have to wait for this virus.

"If it's OK with your father," she says.

"Well, afraid not—we need to catch up on work on the farm," he says.

As usual, Mother buys his lie. Is she really that blinded by her faith? How does she not know what he does to me? What if she does know but she's turning a blind eye because Father has threatened her like he has me? He says if I tell Mom, he will kill me and her both. He even makes a shooting motion with his thumb and index finger sometimes. That scares me. I really need to figure out the combination to the safe, but if he catches me in his room, I'm afraid of what would happen. Does Mom know the combo? If I tell Mom, maybe she will shoot him for me. He's a monster. He has to die. It's his fault more than it is mine or Mom's.

"Don't keep him working all night, Come in before dark." Mother says to Father on her way out the door, Bible in hand. I stare at the floor.

"I won't," Father responds cheerfully. I want to grab a shovel from the barn and beat him with it. I wouldn't stop, not even after he's dead. I would keep pounding his head into the ground until it turns to mush and his skull fractures into pieces all across the carpet. She leaves. He makes me do it twice. Almost back-to-back. Why can't I just live at school?

My head is buried in my pillow when I hear the front door open. Mother has returned home from Bible study. I quickly wipe my face and flip my pillow over to hide where all the tears have made it damp.

"Michael," Mother says, calling for me to come out of my room.

I collect myself and head into the living room, expecting her to tell me what I missed at church. Instead, she tells Father and me something else.

"Well, they aren't sure, but that might be the last time we get to meet for a while. Rumor has it they might be stopping our studies because of the virus. Other places already have. I'm telling you, Frank, I think this could be it. Jesus could come anytime. We ought to be prepared for it just in case he does. I've been putting more and more food down in the storm shelter. If it gets bad enough, we are gonna need to barricade ourselves in there."

"We'll cross that bridge if we come to it," Father says impassively.

He's good at hiding his emotions. I know he's probably seething inside, knowing he won't be able to torture me as easily. I'm good at hiding my emotions, too. I bet I get that from him. I hate that I have any of his traits. I don't want to be anything like him.

"Jesus is coming soon," Mom reaffirms.

How stupid is she? Jesus ain't coming back. I doubt he even came before. And even though it's a dumb idea, it actually wouldn't be the worst thing in the world if we were in the storm shelter. If we were all locked up together, as bad as it would be to have to see him all the time, at least he couldn't do anything because Mother would be down there with us, too. That would be only a temporary solution, though. I have to make it stop forever. No matter what it takes. If I run away, I'm

afraid he will find me. He has to die.

Michael

I've stopped washing my hands at school. If someone coughs near me, I turn in their direction and open my mouth subtly. I touch every surface I can. Hopefully, I can catch this virus soon, so I can give it to Father. I don't think it will kill me, but I kind of hope it does. I'm not even sure I can get it, after what Mom tells me. She says that there have been no reports on the news of kids being infected and that kids might be immune. Why would we be any different, though? I don't understand. The people on TV are idiots. I bet I can get it. I must give it to Father. It's the best chance I've got to get rid of him.

———

A week passes. It's midafternoon between third and fourth period. I reach into my locker and start fumbling around. My locker is a mess. Where is it? I need to find my science book before class starts. A classmate named Teddy opens his locker, which is right next to mine. That's the only reason he starts talking to me.

"Did you hear the good news?" he asks me.

"Huh? Do what?" I say, a little stunned. It's not like he talks to me all the time. It must be something big.

"The good news," he says again.

"Good news?"

"Yeah. Well, it hasn't actually happened yet, but it's going to."

"What's going to?"

"They're going to shut school down. How cool is that?"

"Because of the virus?" I say, recalling the latest from the news my parents make me suffer through. Apparently, kids can catch it now, too. Duh! The supposed experts don't know anything, I swear. They are constantly flip-flopping. One day they say something, and then the next, it's the exact opposite.

I'm surprised I hadn't heard them say anything about schools being canceled, though. Maybe they were saying that during one of the moments I'm staring at the TV and hearing it but totally unaware of what they are actually saying because I'm stuck in the nightmare that is my own head, thinking of past times Father has made me do it and thinking of how it will feel again. I would have figured anything they said about school would have caught my attention, but I guess not. That's how bad it is. If school is canceled, it will only get worse. That's not good news at all. *That's horrible news,* I want to say to Teddy. Instead, I respond with "Oh."

"What do you mean, 'oh'? You actually like coming to school?" Teddy says.

I begin to stumble through my response. "Well, I . . . It's OK. I don't like it, but I

don't—"

"You're such a freaking weirdo," Teddy says, shutting his locker and walking away.

I've found my science book but pretend I'm still looking. I stick my head farther in my locker to hide the tears that are beginning to form in my eyes.

Michael

I've been paying more attention to
the daily press conferences my parents
watch now, but only because I keep waiting
for them to say what I don't want to hear. If
school gets canceled, I'm running away. I'd
have to. It would be unbearable. It would be
just like summertime, when I'm forced to go
work in the field even longer with Father.
Summers are the worst. Sometimes he
makes me do it two or three times a day.
Once or twice in the barn, and then once still
in the evening. It's rare but welcome when
the news conferences about the virus run too

long or when Mother gets too caught up in the news and skips her bath.

Every time they report on something bad, she mutters to herself verses from the Bible. Now I hear her saying, "No weapon formed against us will prosper. No weapon—" I try to tune her out as I watch the idiots on the news conferences tell us ways to stop the spread, one of which is that they we need to stay six feet apart from each other, as they all huddle next to one another shoulder to shoulder around the podium. Am I missing something here? How stupid can you be? You tell us not to get close to one another, but here you all are doing exactly that. Why does it always seem like the dumbest people are always the ones in charge of things? When the news conference ends, Mother starts talking to me about school.

"I wish I didn't have to work. I'd go ahead and pull you out of school right now. I wish we would have homeschooled you from the get-go. Ever since they took God out of the schools, it's not been good. If I thought we could make it with just your dad working on the farm, I'd quit my job, and I'd do it. No more secular lies."

"I don't want to be homeschooled. I like school."

"No kid likes school."

"I do."

"You do?"

I hesitate. I want to say, *Yes I do, because it's my escape.* But I don't. "Mm-hmm" is what I say instead.

———

Another week in hell has passed. I sigh when my alarm goes off and my eyes open. As much as I wish I'd just go to sleep one night and never wake up, I'm quick to get out of bed. I eat quickly so I can get to the bus stop early. I make sure to do this every morning to avoid having to see Father at all. Luckily, he's always out feeding the animals while I'm getting ready for school.

I'm surprised he doesn't make me go with him to help, and then make me do it before school. I don't think he likes mornings much, though.

Mom knocks on my door while I finish getting dressed. I expect her to say what she always says: "You up? Just making sure you're getting ready." She says it every morning, as if it were scripted and as if I have a habit of being late, even though she sees me waiting for the bus while she drives off to work. I'm glad the school is not on her way to work because then I would have to talk to her more. I'm good on that. More religion, more bull crap. No thanks.

"Michael, you don't have to get ready," I

hear her say after a knock, and I immediately know why without asking. "They've canceled school," she says.

I don't say anything immediately. I can't. I'm too stunned at the revelation of how much worse it's going to get. Hell is going to get hotter. It takes everything in me not to tell her right then and there everything that Father does. I can't. I'm too scared of his threats. This is so bad. What if they cancel the remainder of the semester? I can't do it. Something has to give. Either Father has to die, or I do. I don't want to kill myself, but I might not have another choice.

Amber

In the weeks following our decision to get divorced, what little love we had left for each other burned out. A weird mutual respect grew in the process, though. His resentment lessened because he knew he wasn't stuck with me for the rest of his life. We talked about it one night at the house. The only time we have been near each other is when we happen to be eating at the same time because we both like to watch TV while we eat.

I would take my salad to my room but there's no place to set the food down. I say "my room" because he's now staying in the guest room. But here we are, both in the living room. He's heated up a frozen dinner, and I have a salad I picked up at the gas station on the way home from work. He's in his chair eating off his lap as usual, and I'm on the couch with my plate on the coffee table, staring blankly at the screen, when he turns to me out of the blue and says,

"I'll find my own place; you can keep the house."

"Why don't we both find new places and just sell it? Split it fifty-fifty."

"We could, but you can stay if you want. Honestly, I don't mind," he says.

"No, no. It will be good for us both to start fresh somewhere else," I tell him.

"Well, if you don't mind living with me for a while longer, then I guess. I'm sure I could find a place pretty quick, though, and you can stay. Or I could ask my brother if I could stay with him until I find a new place."

"That's not necessary," I say.

"I can look for a place to rent until we can sell the house," he says in between bites.

"I'll look, too."

"If you want."

"And then whichever one of us finds a place first, the other can stay here."

"That works, I guess," he says, wiping his face.

At first, neither one of us does much searching for apartments, though. I've been too busy with work to look. I should have. By the time we both start truly looking, it is too late. The virus is already upon us. It isn't exactly the best time to try to move. Lockdown hits, and we decide to ride it out together.

I had known about COVID-19 back in January, but never in a million years did I think it would become a global pandemic. The chatter among nurses is totally dominated by the virus. No more talks of going out for a drink after work or catching a concert together come the weekend. I miss concerts already. I was supposed to see my favorite—Tim McGraw—next weekend. Instead, it's just going to be home and work on repeat for who knows how long. And talk will be doom and gloom.

I'm on break with a couple of the other nurses who are about to lose their shit just like me. It's hard not to still smell the ER and all its stress, even when we are in the cafeteria surrounded by the scents of whatever today's special is.

"They should pay us more if we have to put our lives in danger like this," Beth says. Petite and pretty, she's usually the one who comes up with ideas, whether it's about getting together to go line dancing or bowling or what the hospital should be doing for us.

"Yeah, they should give us some sort of hazard pay," Tiffany concurs. I know she has all the more reason to worry because she has kids at home.

I keep mostly quiet about it. That's just how I am. I like to assess the situation and let things develop before I jump to any conclusion. My colleagues force my hand, though.

"It's totally ridiculous. We are risking our own lives and the lives of our loved ones if we get sick," says Beth, furthering her point.

"It's just crazy," Tiffany says, then she pauses and turns to me. "What do you think about it, Amber?"

I hesitate. "I-I don't know. I mean, I don't wanna get sick or get my husband sick or any of my friends, but at the same time, being around people who are sick is part of the job" They look at me funny, so I add with a grin, "Getting paid more would be nice, though." That seems to appease them and keep me in the nurse's circle and not totally out on an island by myself.

"Let's hope they do. We should ask them about it," Beth says before taking a big bite of her cheeseburger.

"You go right ahead," Tiffany says.

"I just might do that. I'm not wearing a mask 24/7, though, regardless, I can tell you that right now. Can hardly breathe in those things," Beth says.

I want to point out that she already has to wear them sometimes and that doctors wear them for hours while performing surgery, and they seem to be getting along fine. I don't say that, though. I bite my tongue and nod because I'm not convinced that would be the right thing to say. I feel torn. I want to keep helping people, but I'm afraid of catching the virus and spreading it.

I can't quit my job, though. If I quit, I'll never be able to move out. Shane will find his own place, and then when my savings account runs out, I'll fall behind on the mortgage and be kicked out. Where will I go then?

Chase

Panic and fear began to spread quickly after sports went away and schools began to shut down. I told my boss I didn't feel safe going to the office, but they made it a requirement. I considered quitting right there on the spot after my pleas were denied, but I couldn't afford to. I remember hearing financial advisors say you should have at least six months of funds built up in case of an emergency.

Yeah, well, I'm not guaranteed tomorrow, so I do a piss-poor job of saving. Traveling and buying things are more of a priority. I could last maybe a month if I quit, tops. I did the best I could to stay away from my colleagues for the next week, paranoia rising every time someone got close. Thankfully, my company wasn't completely "dollar signs only." They gave me an out. They released a memo. The part that stuck out to me the most was:

DUE TO THE COVID-19
PANDEMIC, WE WILL BE
ALLOWING ALL EMPLOYEES
TEN COVID-19 PAID DAYS
OFF. YOU WILL RECEIVE
YOUR REGULAR RATE OF
PAY, EQUAL TO WHAT YOU
WOULD RECEIVE FOR A SICK

DAY, BUT THIS WILL NOT
COUNT AGAINST YOUR SICK
DAYS. YOU MAY USE YOUR
COVID-19 FLEX TIME FOR
ANY REASON RELATED TO
COVID-19.

In turn, I sent an email to my boss
that said I would be using my paid time off
to go home to check on my mother. I
explained how she was afraid to leave the
house, so I needed to go home to get her
essential items. Not true, but I wasn't totally
lying. I really was considering going home
to get away from the city. Well over a
million people live in and around Charlotte

compared to fewer than a hundred thousand people in southeast Missouri.

If they are still making people go to the office after two weeks, I will have to make a decision. Financial security versus my health. Health should be an easy choice for me, but there are so many factors to consider. How quickly the cases rise in my county is at the top of the list. If they rise quickly, I'll have to take into account where I would stay if I went home. My dad was never in the picture, so my mom is my only option. I don't feel comfortable asking any friends. Brad is the only person I was close to in that category. He says he is staying in North Carolina regardless.

I'm worried about staying with my mom. She's older—in her early seventies. She's mostly in good health, but they say older people her age are in the high-risk category for death if they contract COVID-19. I don't want to stay with her and risk getting her sick. It would destroy me if I had it, didn't know it and gave it to her, and she died. I wouldn't be able to live with myself. I'm trapped in a horrible conundrum.

I'm sitting on the couch and the TV is on, but I'm not watching it. YouTube has sent me a notification with suggestions for videos I should watch, and before I know it, I'm sucked into a rabbit hole of the top plays of all time from different sports. After several videos, my screen changes. It's my mom calling me. I thought I was in a good place mentally because I was lost in my phone, but that wasn't the case.

"Hi, son."

"Hey, Mom. How ya doing?" I ask.

"I'm fine," she says cheerfully. It was like she didn't know I meant "how are you doing?" regarding the coronavirus. "How are you?"

"I don't know. OK, I guess. We're not going to go to WrestleMania. They are doing it with no fans. I wouldn't go even if they still were."

"Why not? You that worried about the virus?" she asks with a little cheer still left in her voice. I hadn't yet told her about all my fears, so maybe that's why she didn't sound concerned. Then again, I know she has yet to start taking the virus seriously.` I can't say I totally blame her. There are only two cases in her area at this point compared to over a hundred in ours. And damn, man, the positive tests are growing rapidly every day.

"Yes, Mom. You guys don't have it like we have it here. If it keeps getting worse for much longer, I might come home, but I don't want to risk getting you sick. I don't know what to do."

"What about your job?"

"I took time off. They said we could and still get paid if we have any COVID related issues."

"You have an issue? You think you're sick?"

"No, Mom. I'm just trying to be as safe as possible. That's why I took off, so I don't have to be around people. They approved it already."

"Well, that's good you are still getting paid."

"They need to just shut it down and let us work from home, though. It's only a matter of time. They have to," I say, like I'm pleading to them and not talking to my mother.

"Oh, I don't think it's gonna get that bad," she says casually.

"Maybe not there, Mom, because you are in a rural area. There are fewer people. Cities are different. That's why I was saying I want to come home if it keeps getting worse, and I hate to say it, but I think it will. I don't want to risk getting you sick, though. I'd have to stay in the basement," I say, sensing the panic in my voice.

I'm really starting to get annoyed with her lackadaisical approach. Was she that clueless? Was it truly just because she was in a rural area? Was she at the point in her life where she had lived long enough and didn't care whether or not she died? Did she want to die so she could be with other family members who had passed?

"Just come home if you need to," she says with a carefree tone.

"I can't just come home and pretend things are normal. I can't!" I say, starting to lose it.

"Calm down. Calm down. Stop freaking out. It sounds like you're letting the fear get to you. Just come home if you need to. I'll be all right. We will survive."

"Mom! No! You're not listening to me. I'd have to self-quarantine in the basement for fourteen days just to be safe, though, and you couldn't come near me."

"Oh, that's nonsense."

"No, it's not, Mom! They say you can have it for fourteen days and not even know it."

"Who said that?"

"The news. Haven't you been watching the press conferences?" I say, glancing at the TV.

"Not really. I'm surprised you have. I thought you hated the news."

"I do, but this is important. We have to be safe. Please don't go out unless you have to."

"I gotta get groceries."

"No, you don't! Order them online!"

"No, no. Stop yelling," she says, but I can't.

"You don't get it! This is serious!"

"I'm hanging up," she says, and I hear her fumble with the phone.

"Whatever!" I say, and hang up before she does.

I don't talk to her for a week. By then, the number of cases has doubled.

Chase

My company finally got with the program when the stay-at-home order was put into place for everyone. They were basically forced to. That made my decision a little easier, because now if I decided to get out of the city, I could still work, assuming the internet connection is good enough at Mom's. She lives in the boonies, and it's spotty sometimes. Her streaming service will just hang there and buffer for several minutes until you reset it.

There are so many COVID cases here now. I feel like my chances of getting it are pretty good. Sure, I might seem healthy, but I do vape, and I have pretty bad allergies every year as well as silent reflux disease. If I get a sinus infection because of the pollen and then contract COVID, I could be in trouble. It makes me think of my mom and how much I love her and how bad I feel about what happened. I call her to apologize.

"I'm sorry, Mom," are the first words out of my mouth.

"It's OK, sweetie," she says, as though she's already forgiven me. Immediately I feel relieved.

"Thanks, Mom. I shouldn't have blown up on you like that, though."

"It's OK. I forgive you," she says, and that's the end of it, hopefully. But I do want to ask her something related to the virus.

"Mom, I don't wanna fight with you about this virus, but I do have a question that relates to it."

"Go ahead," she says.

"Do you know my blood type?"

"Oh, gosh. No, I sure don't. Why?"

"They think that your blood type could determine how bad the coronavirus will affect you."

"Oh," she says. I can tell she doesn't want to keep talking about it, concerned that we might get into another argument, so I drop it.

"It's OK," I say. I tell her I love her, and she does the same. I really wish I knew what my blood type is, but I didn't want to push it. I think Mom is still fairly relaxed about it all but is beginning to take it a little more seriously as the number of cases goes up there, too, but it's hard to say. I don't ever want to fight with her about it again. We probably would, though, if I moved home. Would I be any safer there? Would Mom? What if it gets really bad there, too? I wanted to ask her more questions while we were on the phone, but I couldn't. I thought about calling her back, but instead I call Brad.

"What should I do, man? Are you gonna stay?" I ask him.

"Yeah, why not? It's going to spread everywhere eventually."

"I just feel like it'd be safer at home in the country with less people."

"Just 'cause there's fewer people doesn't mean anything. It's all about what percentage of people get it."

"You're right, but—"

"Actually, then again, some places they are testing a lot, others not so much."

"That's true."

"And I'm pretty sure it was here long before they started testing anyway," he says.

"Could have—"

"You remember when I got sick last year but tested negative for the flu?"

"Yeah, you think you had corona then?"

"Maybe. Quite possible."

"Well, how come I didn't get it then? We were around each other right before that," I say, thinking back to that time.

"Maybe I didn't have it, or maybe I did. But this whole six-foot crap is a bunch of bullshit. I bet it's a lot harder to catch than you think."

"Yet you think it's going to spread everywhere."

"Eventually."

"I don't wanna find out, man. I really think I should go home. I just wish I knew my mom would stay away from me for fourteen days if I did." I start pacing to work off some nerves.

"You'll be good, dude. Just stay away from her."

"I definitely would."

"Lock yourself in your room and have her slip your food under the door," he says. He doesn't laugh, but I do.

"Where am I gonna piss and shit?"

"Piss in a bucket, and shit on the floor. Then eat that. Your mom won't have to bring you any food," he says, laughing now.

"You're disgusting," I say, laughing again.

It's nice to have a light moment, despite joking about a serious subject. We carry on a little longer, and I don't specifically tell Brad, but I think I've made up my mind.

Chase

I make my way around the side of

the house and down the hill to the

back patio. I pull on

the sliding glass door, and it doesn't budge.

Damnit, she was supposed to have left it

unlocked for me. I look down and see the

long piece of wood keeping the door from

opening still in place. I bang on the glass.

Nothing. I'm left with no choice. I drag my

weary body back up the hill. I'm tired and

just want to crash after such a long drive. I

ring the doorbell twice and step off the front

porch into the grass, giving myself plenty of

room. She opens the door. She starts to come toward me, wanting a hug I'm sure, but I tell her to stay back.

"Take that mask off," she says.

"No, Mom, stay back," I say.

"You're not sick. You look fine."

"I know, Mom. That's not the point. I could still have it and not know it."

"So, you're just gonna lock yourself in the basement for two weeks?"

"Yes. You can't come down. We can't take any chances, Mom. It's just not worth it. Better safe than sorry."

She rolls her eyes at the cliché. "Whatever."

"Not 'whatever'!" I realize I'm starting to get heated again, so I take a deep breath and calm myself. "Look, we can still hang out outside. You can sit on one end of the porch and I can sit on the other end, and we can talk. Then, in fourteen days, if I haven't been showing any symptoms, I'll give you a hug. I'm still keeping my mask on regardless, though."

She smiles and says, "I missed you. I'm glad you're home."

———

So far, so good. One week down, one week to go. I'm surprised Mom is doing so well with it. Is she actually starting to take it more seriously? Or is she just appeasing me? She convinces me to let her cook food and bring it to the stairs where I can grab it and take it back down to my room. I agree, but only with the condition that she allows me to go to the store for her to buy the food. She obliges. I've gone once so far. I wear a mask and stay as far away from people as I possibly can. I get everything she put on the list, including all the ingredients for her homemade biscuits and gravy. She makes the best biscuits and gravy in the world!

That night after dinner we sit out on the porch and talk, keeping our distance, of course. She is probably forty or fifty feet away. I've never been more thankful for that long porch on the front of our house in my entire life. When I start rambling about the coronavirus and different conspiracy theories on how it started, she lets me talk for a little while. Then she was tired of hearing about it.

"Who knows, who knows," she yawns. "I'm sorry, Chase. I'm getting tired. Bedtime," she yawns again.

The first yawn annoys me because I think it was fake, but the second is real.

"Ok, Mom," I say, consenting to the end of our conversation even though I have more to say.

———

I toss and turn all night long. Bad dreams flood my brain. In one, there's a parking garage to my left, but I'm standing in a parking lot looking straight at a hospital—more specifically, the emergency room. I squint to see better, and as I do, I'm sucked through the wall and into the ER. It's empty. There are beds, but no patients. I don't see any doctors or nurses. I scan the room, trying to find someone—anyone. In the back corner, someone is crying and I run to see what is going on. I yank back the curtain, and I see a boy sitting on the edge of a bed. He does not appear to be physically ill, but he is clearly in pain. A nurse emerges from thin air, takes his hand, and begins to comfort him. I want to help, too.

I approach slowly, and it's as if they don't see me yet. I suspect they will soon, but before they do, I hear more cries. This time louder. They are roars of pain. I exit the room and go back into the general area. It's still empty. The sounds are not coming from inside. In an instant, I'm back outside, standing in the parking lot. I look to my left at the parking garage and see a line of

people trying to make their way up to park.
Horns honk, and people yell out their
windows. "Move your cars! My mom is
sick. Move! She needs help." More honks.
Then someone else yells, "Help! Help! My
husband has the virus. He can't breathe. Just
park!" I wonder why they are all trying to
park rather than just pulling up to the
entrance in front. It's empty.

It *was* empty! I realize it is not now
as I turn my head toward more cries and
screams coming from all around me. Sirens
wail, and there are several ambulances
crowding the entrance. EMTs wheel patients
out of the ambulances one by one, as if there
is another dimension inside each ambulance

with an endless amount of space. It's crazy! They keep coming out every few seconds.

I hear someone yelling, "Sir! Sir! Move! Move!" I don't realize it at first, but they are yelling at *me*. I'm in the way. I turn to my right and then turn around. There are doctors and nurses everywhere wheeling in patients on stretchers. Hundreds, if not thousands. "Chase! Chase!" I hear a different voice say. The voice sounds familiar. I dodge to my right, then my left, sprinting back and forth, doing the best I can to not get hit by one of the stretchers. Now I don't feel like I'm actually moving much, as if I am just jerking my arms and legs from side to side. Am I lying down?

"Chase! Wake up!"

I come to. I'm in my bed, and I'm aware now it's my mother who was hollering my name, invading my nightmare, because she is standing over me. She says something, but I don't make out the first part because I'm still half asleep, the remnants of people suffering from COVID still present. I hear the last part of what she says, though. I believe she says, "Don't you have to work? I didn't want you to miss your conference calls." Something like that. I'm not sure. I'm still a little groggy.

Then I'm not! I shoot up out of bed, run to the bathroom, and shut the door. I yell through it, "Mom! What are you doing? You can't be down here. We can't be around

each other, remember?"

"I made breakfast," she says, as if

everything is normal.

Amber

It's getting bad. This virus is ramping up. There's no point in continuing to look for places to rent. It's as if the whole world is frozen. And I'm stuck here with Shane. He's here, but I feel alone. I'm lying in my room, and the TV is on, but it might as well not be. I'm staring at it, but I have no clue what I'm watching due to all the thoughts that circle my mind. I should be sleeping. I need all the rest I can get because work seems to get harder with every shift.

I still kick myself for not doing something different. I see all the various roads I could have taken and where they might have led me, but I didn't take them for reasons I thought were justified at the time. Maybe they were or maybe not. I think about my reasoning for all the big decisions I've ever made and how I got here. I realize some of those reasons were based on things that didn't matter in the long run. At the time, I was so caught up in the moment that I couldn't see the possibility of another future, too worried about fixing a temporary problem with a permanent solution. If it wasn't for my mom, I probably would have made even worse decisions.

She's not here anymore, though. She died of cancer four years ago, and I don't think I've ever taken the time to fully grieve because of everything else that has happened. I wish more than anything that my mother was here to talk to me right now. She was the one I always called when I was feeling stressed out, and this is the most stress I've ever felt in my life. She would know exactly what to say. I'd tell her how I want to quit my job. I can hear her voice in my head. *"You can't do that. You are needed now more than ever. You are strong. You can handle it."*

And I'd believe her because she knew me better than anyone. Even better than Shane did before we started having all our issues with me not being able to have kids. Such a simple little biological abnormality I have no control over led to so much complexity. *"It's not your fault, honey,"* Mom used to tell me before she died. *"It's just the way you were made. Many women are made that way. Not everyone is meant to have a child. I know it's hard to understand and we want to know why, but we don't need to know why because we are not the measure of all things. We just have to accept who we are, understanding that we never had a choice in the matter in the first place. You have plenty of positive attributes you can use to make an impact for yourself, for those around you, and for the world. It doesn't matter how bad we think we have it. The positives are always going to outweigh the negatives. You just have to look for them."*

Her words helped me feel OK with not being a mother for a while, but when she died, I lost sight of that acceptance. I lost sight of who I was, and now I don't know if I'll ever get it back. I miss my mom tremendously. When Dad died of a heart attack ten years ago, I knew she was hurting, but she never let me see it because she knew she had to be the anchor. I wish I had her strength right now, but I'm not her. I don't think I have those qualities. I'm no anchor.

I just wanna lie here and watch TV and never have to go to work again. I want Mom to come in and lie beside me and hold me and tell me everything is going to be OK. She was the best at it. I'd be sobbing, and then she'd start to sing to me, and my tears would go away. Her voice was so beautiful. I do at least have that in common with her. When she was in her last days of fighting cancer, I would stand by her bedside, hold her hand, and sing the very same songs she used to sing to me. Songs by Tim McGraw, Brooks & Dunn, George Strait, and other country legends. I hoped somehow they would bring her back to life or at least provide some comfort for her if she could hear me. I may not have been able to save her, but I knew that wasn't my fault. I did everything I could. I made her feel as comfortable as possible.

Now I just have to keep going to help other people. No matter how hard it is, I have to keep hearing her voice in my head telling me I'm strong. And even though I don't think I am, I have to convince myself that it's true. If I pretend long enough, maybe somehow I will be.

Chase

Mom and I meet on the porch for dinner, her at one end and me at the other, as we've done just about every night since I've been back. It feels diffcrent now, though.

"Mom, you shouldn't have gotten so close to me. It's spreading bad. More and more people are dying every single day. I won't lose you. I can't."

"I'm sorry. I thought you had to work, though, and you were missing your conference calls."

"No, Mom. They are different each day. I didn't have one till eleven today.

That's why I was sleeping in. You can't do that, Mom! You can't get too close."

"Won't happen again," she says. I'm not sure I believe her because I think I was wrong about her changing. She's still not taking it seriously, even after I thought she was starting to come around.

The following evening there's no arguing, just me worrying. There's more worry the next night, and I feel it's only going to get worse for a while. Ever since she got too close to me when she woke me from my nightmare, I fear it will become a reality. Time couldn't move any slower right now.

I watch both nights of WrestleMania, and man, it is weird seeing them wrestle with no fans in the arena. It's just silence other than the announcers and the wrestlers talking smack to each other. It sucks knowing that particular bucket-list item will continue to go unchecked, but right now I don't really care. At eleven days into my stay, I breathe easier, knowing we are closer to the fourteen-day window when they say it can be spread. But how do they really know? It could be shorter; it could be longer. This virus is too new. They are learning more and more every day.

I feel fine, so I hope she's fine. I'd have to be sick to spread it to her, right?

They say on the news it's possible you
might have it and not know it and still give it
to someone. But how could they possibly
know that if the people who are spreading it
don't even know they're sick? There would
be no way of knowing, no way of tracing it,
would there? It's not like you can just test
for it and get the results back instantly. It
takes days, weeks even, from what I
understand. It just doesn't make sense to be
able to spread it unless you have a fever. It
should be like other viruses, shouldn't it? Or
is it really that much worse, that different
from all the others? If it is true that you can
have it but not know it, then I need to
assume that I have it all the time and be even

101

more careful than I am already to not get anyone else sick. But what if it's too late?

On day twelve as we sit down with our food, the breeze catches my napkin and whisks it off my plate and into the yard. I get up, set my plate down in the chair next to me, and run to retrieve it. I sit back down.

"You could have just gone in and gotten another one; it's not that big of a deal," my mother says to me.

"No, Mom, not until fourteen days have passed. Maybe longer."

She hisses at me and rolls her eyes. "Longer?"

"Yes, Mom. Maybe we should just keep staying away from each other until the numbers start going down. If everybody would just stay at home, hopefully it will be over sooner rather than later."

"I'm not going to live in fear," she says emphatically.

"I'm not saying you should, but right now we need to be smart."

"I know, I know. You've told me."

"We do. Are you feeling OK today?"

"I'm fine," she says, and I believe her.

———

I ask her again the next night.

"I'm fine," she says, then she coughs. I don't believe her.

"Are you sure, Mom?" I ask her several more times throughout the meal, as she coughs more frequently. With each cough comes another wave of fear.

"Going in. Good night," she says quickly, and I notice she's barely eaten any of her food. She must have been nibbling at it or pretending to eat it.

"Mom, wait," I say, rising from my chair, plate still in hand. I take a few steps toward her, but she doesn't turn toward me, and I hear her say she loves me as she opens the door. She goes in, and I run to the door. I knock softly at first, then louder when she doesn't answer.

Finally, she says something. "Go to bed, Chase. We are supposed to stay away from each other, remember?"

I ask her if she's OK several more times, and she says yes, again telling me to go to bed. Eventually, I oblige. I go through the back door, take off my clothes and lie in bed, my eyes wide open. All the waves of fear seem to have formed an ocean, and I feel like I'm drowning in them. I start to shake and take long deep breaths to try to calm myself. There will be no nightmares tonight because I don't think I will be able to sleep. *"Supposed to stay away from each other, remember?"* Her voice echoes in my head, and I know she isn't saying it this time to mock me. She wants to protect me from her.

Michael

I'm afraid we will never go back to school. They want us to start doing virtual classes, but that won't help my situation any. Today will be the same as the previous day, though it feels like each one is getting worse. I act like I'm sleeping as long as I can. I flinch when I hear him enter my room.

I flinch again when he nudges me to make me get out of bed.

"Come on. Got some work in the barn I need you to help me with," Father says.

"Have a good day, boys," Mother says. "Off to work I go. Lucky you, Michael. Farmwork is not as bad as school, I wouldn't think. I assume I'll never have to stop working. People will always need to go to the grocery store, even if it's only to pick up an order. People will always need food, so your dad's job and mine are safe. We are blessed. One day at a time until he returns." Then she starts to sing, "Jesus is coming soon; Jesus is coming soon."

As soon as she's out the door and her car is out of sight, I'm gonna make a run for it. I've decided I don't care if he finds me. I have to try.

———

She's gone. "Let's go," Father says.

"I-I'll be out there in a minute. Go ahead. I need to change into my overalls," I somehow manage to say to him.

"Hurry up!" he yells at me, evil in his eyes.

I go to my room and stand at the door until I hear the front door close. I race to the window, hiding behind the curtains and watch as he enters the barn. I race back to my room, dump out my schoolbooks from my backpack, throw open my dresser drawers, and begin to fill my backpack with clothes. It gets full quickly—too full. I go to zip it up, and the zipper breaks. There's no time to fix it, no time to find anything else to put my stuff in. I have to go. He will be back any minute to look for me.

I turn to go out my door, when I notice my favorite book on top of my dresser: *The Sign of the Beaver*. I think of how I will be just like Matt, learning to survive without my family. I scoop it up and put it in my back pocket. I turn back toward the door, then begin to run through the hallway. I smack right into someone and fall to the ground. My backpack went flying as I fell, items scattering on the carpet. It's Father. I scurry away from him back near my room and get to my feet, as he stands there blocking my path of escape.

"Where do you think you're going? I had a feeling you might do something stupid, so that's why I came back in. You think I don't know you, boy? You ain't going *nowhere*. Guess we don't have to go to the barn right now, after all. Go to your room and get ready!"

"No!" I yell at him. He's shocked.

The only other time I told him no was when

it first started happening, but when he

pinned me against the wall and put the full

weight of his body on me, it was almost

impossible to breathe. "Do it, or you won't

be breathing at all," he'd said. I didn't want

to die then, so what was I supposed to do

except succumb to his sick, twisted,

perverted ways? Now that I don't care about

dying anymore, things are different.

"What did you say?" he says, taking

a step closer.

"No! I won't do it anymore! You'll

just have to kill me."

"You will to do it!" he screams at me.

"No! Just kill me!" I say, sounding as if I'm begging him to end my life.

He advances toward the door. Though I say I want to die, at the moment he lunges to grab me, I instinctively duck and scurry around him and down the hall. I don't have my backpack with any of my clothes or anything else, but it doesn't matter, I'll still be free soon. I know where I'll go—straight to the police station to tell them everything. I'm at the front door, but he has locked it, and I don't get it open in time. He grabs me from behind and turns me around. His face is as red as Satan himself. He punches me straight in the face with a hard right hand.

Then he does it again. I fall to the ground

against the door, and he pounds his fists into

my sides now. There's so much pain. I can't

tell where it's coming from, my head or my

sides. Blood gushes from my face. "Stop!

Stop!" I yell at him, but he doesn't. His fists

keep coming.

Michael

I'm too weak to resist him anymore. He finally stops. He carries me over his shoulder to my room and throws me on my bed. Pain shoots through my entire body. I'm too weak to move. He exits my room, then returns with a towel to wipe the blood off me and a fresh set of linens to change my bed.

"I swear to God if you tell your mother about this, I will actually kill you next time and her, too. We're going to have to come up with something. We can . . . we can . . . Let's tell her you were in with the

steers and one of them attacked you. That's
what you will tell her. You'll tell her that. It
will work. She's too naïve to know the
difference. Got it?"

"OK," I whisper.

When he's done wiping the blood off
me, Father takes the stained towel and
throws it under my bed. He pushes me to the
floor and changes the bed sheets.

"I'm going to let you rest for a
couple of hours, but then you're gonna get
your ass back up and come help me. I'm
gonna tough it out, and you are, too."

I say nothing, and he leaves the
room. I try to go back to sleep, but I'm in
too much pain. I lie there and stare emptily

115

at the ceiling, trying not to move. He comes back in for lunch. He hollers at me once before he's finished eating and then again when he's done. I hear him coming for me now. I wince as I turn my body away from the door to pretend once more that I am sleeping. "Get up! Time to get back to work. Let's go!"

I don't want him to shake me, so I turn over gingerly and face him.

"I can't. I'm too weak."

He must see in my eyes that I'm not lying because he doesn't argue. He knows what he's done, how hard he hit me.

"Fine, you're useless anyway," he says.

He slams my door, and a few seconds later, I hear him slam the front door as well. An hour later he comes to my room to make sure I'm still there, that I hadn't run away. How could I? I can barely walk. I keep my eyes closed until I hear the door shut again.

Another hour passes. I hear the front door creak once more. I close my eyes and wish him away. I hear a voice, but it's not his. It's hers. The voice of a savior. It's Mother. It sounds like she is on the phone. "They are going down to just one girl in the afternoons now because of the virus, so my hours got cut," I hear her say. That's why she is home. The coronavirus might just be

117

the best thing that ever happened. I hear her say goodbye to whoever she was on the phone with. I struggle to sit up, but once I am up, I yell her name as best I can.

"Mom!"

"Michael, why aren't you outside helping—" Concern hits her as she notices my face. "Oh my God, Michael, what happened? My baby. What happened to you?"

"Does Dad know you're home?" I say, thinking on my toes.

"No. He must be in the barn. What happened to you? Are you OK?"

"Are you sure?"

"Am I sure of what? Please tell me what happened to you," she says as she gently touches my face. I try not to wince in pain. I try to stay focused.

"Does Dad know you're here?" I ask again, wanting to know with one hundred percent certainty.

"No, baby. Why?"

I pause to reconsider when the shame hits me. I've been waiting so long to tell her, but it's so bad. I don't know if I can bring myself to do it.

"What is it, baby?" Mom asks. "Look at me," she says. "What happened to you? Please tell me."

She's crying, and I can't hold it in any longer. Finally, after years of suffering in silence, the words leave my mouth.

"It was him, Mom. He beat me. He. . . he makes me do awful things to him, and I couldn't do them anymore. Mom, we need to get out of here. He said he would kill us if I told you. We-we need to go," I cry.

"What? I-I don't understand," she says, shaking her head rapidly.

Slowly, with as little detail as possible, I tell her what he makes me do. It's hard to talk through all the emotional pain, and physical pain as well. Tears pour down my face with each word.

"He-he couldn't do that. He's your father. How could he—" She stumbles over her words in disbelief; she's trembling. Shock and anger are written all over her face.

"It's true, Mom. Why would I lie to you?"

I search her face, hoping with all my heart she will believe me. She gathers her thoughts, and then her face changes.

"That's why—" She stops to gather her thoughts again.

"That's why *what*, Mom?"

"That's why you are the way you are. There's nothing wrong with you. It's him. He's made you this way, hasn't he?"

I try to say yes, but I start crying again before any words can come out. She believes me!

"Wait right here," she says. She's stopped shaking and is eerily calm.

"But we have to go now, Mom. Now!" I yell as she walks away. She storms off to her room, and I stumble out of my room and to the living room window to make sure he isn't coming. I turn as Mother comes back into the living room; in her hands is the shotgun I've wanted to get a hold of for so long.

She clutches it tightly and looks squarely at me, fiercely intent.

"What you told me is one hundred percent true? Word for word?"

"Yes, Mom." I say, wiping tears from my face.

"OK. Then he shall pay for his sins. An eye for an eye."

"What are you going to do?"

"Stay here and lock the door behind me."

I watch as she holds the butt of the weapon to her right shoulder and points it toward the barn as she walks. Then, a few moments later, I hear the bullet leave the gun.

Chase

From the top of the basement steps, I holler through the door. Maybe all she needed was a good night's sleep. *Maybe she's all better today,* I think wishfully. She should be up by now, though. I hear no sounds coming from the kitchen this morning. I put my ear to the door. I hear no sounds coming from anywhere. "Mom! Are you OK?" I yell. "Mom!" Nothing. I turn around and stumble, putting my hand against the wall so as not to fall as I run down the steps. I grab my mask and slip it on before running back up the steps. I pause at the door and yell once more. "Mom! Are you up?"

Still nothing. I have no choice. I'm going in. I fling open the door. The bathroom door to the right is open, and the lights are off, I notice, so I know she's not in there. I glance at the kitchen before going down the hall to her room. Her door is open, the lights are off, and there she is. She's lying on her side with her back toward me. I stand at her doorway.

"Mom," I say gently. Nothing. "Mom, wake up," I say in a normal tone this time. She doesn't move. I begin to panic and run to her side. I reach down. "Mom, please wake up," I say, shaking her shoulder. I hear her cough, and she rolls over. *Thank God!* I couldn't help but think the worst, even though I don't think the virus kills you that quickly. "Good morning," she says groggily.

"How are you feeling?" I ask, already knowing the answer because she does not look good. Her face is shaded differently and not nearly as bright without her usual cheerful energy.

"I've got a pretty bad headache," she says. "Can you get me some Tylenol, please?" she says, sitting up slightly before rubbing her temples.

"I think we should take you to the hospital," I say, but she brushes it off.

"I'm fine. Just get me some Tylenol."

I sigh. "Where is it?"

"Still second shelf, bathroom cabinet," she says weakly.

I knew that, but I'm not thinking clearly. As I scan the shelf, I realize I didn't ask her how many she wanted, so I just grab the entire bottle and take it to her. "How many do you need?"

"Better give me three or four. It's pounding," she says, and I notice the pain in her eyes as she opens and closes them every few seconds. "Let me go get you some water," I say. When I come back from the kitchen with it, she shovels four pills into her mouth, puts the glass to her lips, and gulps. She lies back down and closes her eyes again.

"Can I get you anything else, Mom?"

"Better grab the thermometer; I'm pretty sure I've got a fever." She puts her palm to her forehead. "Should be in one of the drawers in the bathroom."

I struggle to find it at first, but after shuffling through items in the second drawer, I feel and see it at the same time. Back in the bedroom, I take the cap off for her. She takes it from me and sticks it under her tongue. We wait. *Please let it be normal,* I say to myself. It finally beeps at us. Three times. Oh, no. That means she's got a fever.

"What is it?" I say.

"Not good," she says.

"What's the temperature?"

"High."

"Mom, please."

She doesn't say anything, but instead, hands it to me. It's blank.

"It already disappeared. What was it? Just tell me."

"One-oh-three," she says.

"Mom! We need to get you to the hospital or at least call the doctor."

"I'll be fine. Let the Tylenol kick in. It'll go down."

It doesn't. Her fever is nearly the same when I check it with her that afternoon and then again in the evening.

She sleeps most of the day. I bring her a fresh, cold rag every hour or so. I don't want to, but I leave her briefly to go to the store to get her some chicken noodle soup. She barely touches it. I'm extremely worried. I hope I didn't get anyone else at the store sick, but she has to eat, and she didn't want anything else. I'm starting to think maybe I got her sick after catching it at the store when I first got home rather than catching it from someone back in North Carolina. Too much time has passed since then. I feel fine, though. It really doesn't seem likely that I gave it to her, but I still feel guilty. *It had to be someone else,* I think. But how? Did she go out and I didn't know it? It doesn't make sense.

I could still end up getting sick, though, and if I do, I might not be able to take care of her. She could die, and I could die, too. I try to forget about all my fears, telling myself it wouldn't be that bad for me. I'm young and healthy. I should be fine, but what if I'm not? She's definitely not, but she's older and vulnerable, more susceptible to illness, and it's coming to fruition. I'm so scared. I can't think like that. No, God. Please let her get better now.

Day two she is no better but still refuses to go to the hospital. On day three, she's gotten worse. She's having trouble breathing, and though I know she is still going to fight me, I have to take her to the hospital, into my nightmare. I wonder how my dream would have ended. Maybe the doctors and nurses would have healed them all. Maybe it would have turned into a happy dream. I must believe that it will. I must believe Mom will get better. Mom will get better. Mom will get better. *God, please let her get better.*

Chase

I should have taken her yesterday,
but I let her talk me out of it again. As I
wake up on the morning of day four, I'm
still feeling fine, but if Mom is no better
when I check on her in a minute, I don't care
what she says, I'm taking her. I put on my
mask and make my way to her room,
praying every step of the way that she will
be feeling better. I enter her room. Oh, God.
She's worse. She's worse. We have to go.

"Mom, I've got to get you to the
hospital right now," I say, beginning to
panic.

"N-No. I'll be all right," she says, wheezing.

"Mom, you can barely talk," I say, trying to hide my fear.

"Just let me rest. I just need rest."

"Mom! I'm taking you now."

"I'm good," she says, sounding like she's choking.

I'm about to lose it. Not from anger but from fear. "Mom! Please." Tears begin to form and then are down my cheeks before I get out my next sentence. "I don't want you to die. Please, just let me take you. Please. Please."

She doesn't say anything. I think I've exhausted her more with my pleading.

She closes her eyes and rolls over in bed. I sit by her side and watch her sleep. Her snores, wheezes, and unconscious little coughs are so bad, I feel I'm left with no choice. I know she's going to be mad at me, but I also know in my heart it's the right thing to do. It's the *only* thing to do if I want her to live. I head to the kitchen, then stand between the sink and the table. I reach into my pocket, pull out my phone, and hit the dreaded three numbers no one ever wants to press.

An ambulance takes longer to arrive than I would have liked. I open the door, and they wheel in a stretcher. She wakes, hearing them preparing all their gear.

"What is this?"

"Mom, you're going to the hospital. I'm sorry. You have to."

I'm surprised when she doesn't fight me about it. Maybe she wants to but doesn't have the strength. I am by her side every step of the way as they lower the stretcher and slide her off the bed onto it. They put an oxygen mask on her and then carefully wheel her out of the house and down our brick sidewalk, which leads to a circle driveway. I stand out of the way as they load her up, then begin to climb into the ambulance.

"Wait, sir. You can't ride in there with her. I'm sorry," says one of the paramedics, his words a bit muffled through his mask.

"Why?" I ask, but before they answer, I say, "I'll just follow you to the ER, then."

"I'm afraid you can't do that either, sir."

"What do you mean?"

"No one is being allowed inside right now unless they are a patient. It's due to COVID-19 protocols."

"B-but . . . I have to be with her. I have to make sure she's going to be OK." I'm beginning to panic.

"You can call and check on her in an hour or so once we get her admitted."

"That's . . . that's bullshit."

"I'm sorry, sir. Please step away from the doors."

"But—"

"Step back," the paramedic says, and I have no choice as he begins to shut the door.

I get out of the way so they don't hit me with the doors. I start to cry again as I watch them wheel her away. I drop to my knees and take off my mask. I wipe tears from my eyes and wonder if I'll ever see her again.

Amber

People come in all the time with coughs, fevers, chills, shortness of breath, and other similar symptoms, and the positive tests are adding up quickly, despite the measures put in place weeks ago to try and stop this virus. An entire section of the ICU has now been dedicated solely to COVID patients. I'm glad I'm not in that section, but with the numbers rising daily, I fear it will only be a matter of time before my section has one, too.

Having to take care of more patients by myself because so many nurses are specifically working in the COVID ward is difficult. If I'm assigned to take care of COVID patients as well, my job will become that much harder. The projections don't look good. It's crazy to think about all the possibilities. For now, they are just what-ifs and maybes, and I can't focus on that. I have to do my job and just be as safe as I can. Head down. One foot in front of the other.

———

Within two weeks, we have more COVID patients in the ICU than we do people with other issues. We wear masks and shields over those masks, and it's hard to tell who's who and who's supposed to be doing what with all the protective equipment we have on. It's chaos. The first COVID patient in our section multiplies quickly. Soon we have our first death and then more. They add up quickly. It hits me hard, but there is little time for sympathy or processing what is happening. I knew seeing death was part of the deal when I signed up to be a nurse, but this is different. It's overwhelming because of how often it is happening and how the number of deaths seems to increase with each shift.

The days seem to come and go in a haze, maybe because I'm constantly exhausted. Or maybe because they are virtually all the same, each day chaotically in sync with the last. They feel the same because, well, madness is madness. At the same time, each day is different from the last because we don't know what to expect from this virus. It's still too new. It seems like what we think it is and how we think we should deal with it keeps shifting under us.

I continue to try my best to just focus on the task I am given. And right now, that's dealing with an older lady named Evelyn, who I'm not sure is going to make it. She's been here a few days now and is gradually getting worse. I've ordered chest X-rays and blood work, and it looks like she's going to have to be put on a ventilator soon. She can barely answer my questions with a yes or no, so I try not to ask many, which goes against what I normally do.

I like to get to know each patient if I can, so I ask them about their families, their jobs, their hobbies. I want to know them because their lives are in my hands. And I hope answering my questions will help them think about something other than being stuck in a hospital bed. I may not know much about her because she's barely able to talk, but I can see the softness in her eyes—a glimpse into who she is. I can feel the positive energy of her soul. I don't want her to die, but I have to wonder if she will be here for my next shift. I worry for her, and then I worry again about me. It's a constant flow of anxiety.

As soon as I get Evelyn cleaned up, another twelve-hour shift will be over. I should be able to sleep when I get home because of my exhaustion, but that's not always the case. My body might be worn out, and you'd think my brain would be, too, but a million thoughts run through it when I try to sleep. I often feel as if my body is asleep and I am unable to move, yet somehow my brain keeps moving. It's as if I'm asleep but awake at the same time. I'm in a modified dream state, reliving everything I'm going through. Will she die?

Will I die if I catch it, or will I get Shane

sick? It's probably not *if* but more like *when*.

It's coming, isn't it? I can't go

untouched, can I? There's no way. Not with

my job. It's only a matter of time. I'm in the

middle of the COVID storm.

Chase

I've tried calling several times. Each time they barely tell me anything. After each call, my brain runs in circles as I try to understand how it happened. If I did catch the virus at the store, how exactly did that happen? I thought I'd done everything right. I still think that's how it happened, though, and that I gave it to her when she woke me, thinking I had to be up for a work conference. It baffles me, though. I mean, I did hear someone coughing an aisle over from me, but it couldn't have traveled through the shelves. Could it?

I know that seems stupid, but I find I'm asking myself those questions all the time now because I don't know what to believe. Did it go over the shelves? It couldn't have, right? The contagion would have fallen to the ground, not traveled up. I saw a lady coming toward me when I was looking at cereal, but I grabbed my Cap'n Crunch before she got close, didn't I? I'm pretty sure I did. I thought I did. No one got close to me that I can remember. Wait. I thought I could feel someone a little too close when I was in line, but I didn't want to turn around to look and have them breathe in my face. Could that have been it?

Did the virus get on one of the products I bought? Did the lady checking me out have it on her hands because she was touching all the different products from each person and handling the money people gave her? Did I then touch it, get the virus, and not know it? Did Mom get it from me? Or maybe she got it from touching something I bought at the store. Does the virus stay on surfaces that long?

Why did she have to come down into the basement and be around me? I don't blame her, though. I blame myself. I should never have moved home. It was selfish. I should have stayed by myself and not exposed her. How could I have been so dumb? If she dies, I will never forgive myself. I've now tested positive, too, but I don't have any symptoms. I would do anything to trade places with her right now. She does not deserve this. Why can't I see her? If we both are infected, it shouldn't matter, right? Maybe the doctors and nurses are worried she will get me sick even though I already technically have it, or maybe they are worried that I could make her sicker since I'm the one who gave it to her in the first place. I'm not sure how it works. I don't think they do, either. It's all a guessing game right now. They are learning on the fly, just like we are.

Amber

Evelyn is on a ventilator when I arrive the next day. I check her vitals. They are bad, but they go unchanged for hours. With the help of another nurse who lifts her legs and arms, I wipe her off with my cleaning towel. We then call in a CNA to help gently turn her over on her side to prevent bedsores. Even a simple task such as this is complex. If we don't do it just right, with special care, her blood pressure could drop, her oxygen levels could plummet, her heart could stop. It may not matter soon, but it is still our responsibility to make sure she is cared for. I care deeply about people. I care about *her*. Despite every thought that tries to pull me under, I am strong. I will push on and do my job as long as it takes to get out of this thing, as long as it takes for life to return to normal, then I can worry about how to settle my divorce and be on my own. No matter how long, no matter what it takes. On my count, we turn Evelyn slowly, and her vitals stay the same for now.

I drag my body through another long shift. I stay fifteen hours this time because one of our nurses has quit to be a traveling nurse, going to work at other hospitals even worse off than ours. I don't blame her. I know she will probably get double the pay, meaning she'll get what we are worth. I press on without her. I don't think of leaving. Not right now.

I think about whether there is anything I could possibly do to save Evelyn's life. But I can't do anything to save her. I can only comfort her, be there for her when her family can't. She's not going to make it. I've finally accepted that now, just as I did for the other patients I've seen go, each taking a small part of me with them. I now know why she stands out from the rest, though. It's because she reminds me of my own mother. I didn't realize it before because they don't look anything alike or even have the same hair or eye color, but the way she looked at me while she still could was the same way Mom did before she died four years ago from cancer. The softness, the kindness, the love, slowly slipping away.

She doesn't have a family member here to hold her hand as she crosses over, so I know it is my duty. What an awful thing for people to have to die alone. I wonder if it's as bad as feeling isolated for most of your life. Here she is in this windowless world, about to be taken to the next. I'll hold her hand for as long as it takes until she is gone. I take it and begin to sing the same song I sang to my mother, "Live Like You Were Dying" by Tim McGraw. I ad-lib and say "flying," though, instead of "dying."

Then all of a sudden, I feel pressure. She's squeezing my hand. Then she releases it. I keep singing. A minute passes, and then she squeezes it again. I sing a little louder. I look at her vitals. They've improved ever so slightly. She stops squeezing. Her vitals hold steady and stop declining. Then she squeezes my hand again even harder. Her vitals improve once more. Her body temperature is normalizing, as well as her pulse, respiration rate, and blood pressure. I take my free hand and put it over my face as I use my thumb to wipe tears from my left eye and my index finger to wipe them from my right eye. She squeezes my hand again. Then again. Each time longer and with more strength. I never stop singing. After twenty

minutes, I'm still holding on as she lifts her

arm to her side. I look at her, and her eyes

are open. They are as soft as ever. She's

coming back to life. Her vitals are

miraculously all within normal range. I

know without a shadow of a doubt that she

is going to make it.

Michael

Father is dead, and Mother is in jail. She confessed right after it happened. She walked right by me, back into the house as I stood there in shock. She picked up the phone, and all she said was, "I murdered my husband." Then she told them her name and address. She went to the couch and stared at the floor. I just stood there and looked at her. She was totally numb, and so was I. I couldn't believe that all it took to get rid of that monster after so long was me telling her. In that moment, though, I didn't think much about the lasting effect. It was hard to process everything I was feeling. All I could do was stand there and look at her in disbelief. She showed no emotion.

A few minutes later we heard the sirens, and she looked up. She said, "He's gone. I love you." And that was it. The next thing I knew, authorities came through the front door with guns drawn. They put her hands behind her back, handcuffed her, and led her out the door. One of the police officers stayed inside with me.

"Are you OK?" he said.

"I thought I would be," I managed. I wasn't sure how to feel. He asked me what happened, but all I could say was, "She shot him."

A little while later, I went with him, and then eventually they took me to the DCS office. They asked about relatives and who I might be able to stay with. I told them I had no extended family around.

All my grandparents are dead. I have no aunts or uncles or anyone else. I do have some distant relatives, but they live way out in California. They aren't going to take me. I'm wanted by no one.

—

I've been here in this big foster house with seven other kids I'm supposed to call my brothers and sisters for a couple of weeks now. I've had a lot of time to think and process everything that happened in such a short time. I think I am happy Father is dead. I should be, but it's very weird. No matter how crazy Mom is about her beliefs, I don't want her to end up locked away. I imagined myself sticking it out with her until after high school, but that's not going to happen now. It's not how I thought it would go down, but I'm happy to have escaped. Knowing I will never again have to do any of those horrible things Father made me do gives me a little hope. Thank God for the pandemic and Mom coming home that day. Otherwise, I would still be trapped.

It's not so bad here, except for my foster parents making us wear masks all the time unless we are in our room. I share a room with another boy about my age. At first, I mostly ignored him, put my headphones on, and listened to music like I always used to do, but he's talked me into playing this old board game called backgammon with him, and as stupid as I thought it was at first, it's actually pretty fun.

I thought it was some version of checkers, but it's not. It's kind of like it, but not really. You do have checkers, but you roll the dice to move your pieces around the board and safely to the other side. As long as you have more than one checker on a spot,

you're safe. It's when one becomes isolated,

on a spot by itself, exposed to the danger of

being knocked off the board by your

opposition and sent back to the middle—to

the abyss, to have to start all over again—

that you have to worry.

Those are the best times—when it's

just me and him and not the whole bunch.

They are all OK. It's just a little bit

overwhelming is all, but it'll do for now.

Five years and counting, then I'll be

eighteen, and I can move out and start a life

of my own. It would be cool if I got a good

home sooner, but I know no one will want to

adopt me because I'm too old. They want babies or just past the baby stage, where they don't have to deal with wiping asses and changing diapers.

There's only one baby here in this house. Despite all of us foster kids, it's mostly silent at night after everyone has gone to bed, except occasionally the baby girl will begin to cry. Then one of my foster parents will go to help her, perhaps changing her diaper. It does not distract me much from my thoughts, though. Most nights I lie on my bed unable to sleep until well past midnight. Inevitably, I think of the past. It still haunts me, but I'm beginning to heal. I think that one day I might be able to help others who are going through, or have gone

through, the same things as me. I think I'd

like to write a book about it one day.

Chase

Earlier this week, I called the hospital again, expecting to be told— again—that Mom is still fighting. Instead, the voice on the other end told me she's doing a little better. They said she almost died but that she didn't, and it now seems that she is going to pull through. *"Almost died. Almost."* That hits me hard. I was that close to losing her.

This time when I call, the receptionist asks if I want to speak to her. I'm so surprised, I don't answer right away.

"Sir?" she says.

"Yes, please. I would love to talk to her," I say, and a minute later she's on the phone.

"Hi, Chase," she says softly.

"Mom, how are you? Are you OK?" I say, trying to hide my emotions because I'm crying now.

"I'm a whole lot better now," she says.

"That's . . . that's . . . They said you almost died. I don't know what I would do without you, Mom," I manage to choke out.

"It's OK, baby," she says, hearing my sniffles.

"It's my fault, Mom. It's all my fault."

"It's—"

"I should have been more careful. I—"

"Chase. Stop. Listen. It's not your fault. It's mine," she says, and even through the phone, I can feel the guilt hit her.

"It's not. I should have stayed farther away from people."

"No, Chase. I went to the store."

"What?"

"You forgot to get butter."

"You did? When? Why would you do that, Mom? I could have gone back."

"Yes. I'm sorry. You were still sleeping."

"Why didn't you wake me up?"

"I just ran up to the milk store real quick. I didn't think it would be a big deal. I didn't plan on being in there very long, but then I ran into a lady in my book club, and I talked to her for a few minutes about how *Emma in the Night* ended. It was stupid. Not the book. The book was great, but *I* was stupid. I realize that now, but it had been weeks since our last meetup, and we just got to talking like everything was normal. I realize it's not now. I'm sorry, Chase. I should have listened to you sooner."

"It's OK, Mom. You didn't know. You wanted life to be like it's always been. I understand."

"It's not, though, Chase. I see that now. I'm sorry I didn't believe you."

I tell her again that it's OK and take in what she said and what I just said, and I wonder. How long will it take? Will life ever be normal again?

.

Amber

I worked three straight weeks

without a day off. Although the hospital is

so short-staffed, I am told to take today off.

My supervisor must have seen how drained I

am and realized that if I didn't try to rest

some, I would be of no use to anyone. I'm

thankful for the day off, yet I feel as if I

should be there, caring for my patients,

trying to save as many people as I can at the

hospital.

I don't know what to do with myself.

I try to sleep in but have no luck. I lie in bed

till well past noon, staring at my phone,

reading various news articles about the virus, and then watching Netflix. Eventually I leave my room and come down to the kitchen. I see Shane sitting in the living room watching *Seinfeld* reruns.

We used to watch *Seinfeld* together all the time, but I don't want to get close to him now. The truth is, I just don't feel right watching anything with him anymore, regardless of the virus. I don't feel right saying much to him at all.

If we were still together, I'd sit with him until a commercial came on and then tell him about everything that's going on at work and how hard it is. I'd tell him about my life, anticipating the kind words he would say to me to help me through it. He always seemed to know what to say to me when I was stressed. He helped me release my tensions with elegance and ease.

But I can't do that now. I don't want to burden him with my troubles. I don't want to hear his words. I know he would still know what to say, despite all we've been through, but I can't. It wouldn't feel right at all. It would be nice to talk to someone about it all, though, to help ease the stress. He's just not the right person anymore.

—

When I arrive at work the next day, Evelyn is not here. A sick feeling clutches my gut when I go to ask about her. Did she suddenly decline again and not make it this time?

"She was discharged."

"So soon?" I say. I'm shocked. Normally it takes a lot longer than that. Shocked, but overjoyed. I do wish I could talk to her, to tell her how happy I am that she pulled through. To figure out how. But all that matters is that she's OK. That she's going to make it. The shift is still tough, as not one but two new patients have replaced

Evelyn. Yet somehow, despite the

circumstances that should make it my most

difficult shift yet, I feel a sense of relief. I

feel an even deeper calling. The deepest I've

ever felt since this whole mess started. If I

helped save her, I can save more. Not

everyone who comes in with COVID has to

die.

I'm feeling a sense of pride when I

arrive home, knowing I'm making a

difference. That gives me a little energy. I'm

not as completely exhausted as I was before.

Then I hear groaning coming from the

bedroom. It's Shane. It sounds like a cry for

help. I rush to the doorway. I look at him. He is shivering. He is pale. My heart sinks.

———

A few days have passed, and we've both tested positive. I'm asymptomatic, one of the lucky ones. My husband, however, is not so fortunate. He's still sick. I don't get it. He's the poster boy for what a healthy person should look like. He eats right; he works out daily. He doesn't drink; he doesn't smoke. He does all the right things. Yet here he is, stuck in bed, hot one minute and cold the next.

I hear him moaning, and I go in to check on him. "Slow, deep breaths. It's OK. You're going to be all right," I say, realizing deep breaths aren't exactly coming easy for him at this moment. I fear he will have to be admitted to the hospital soon. I care for him as if I were on the clock, but I don't have everything I need here. I hate this.

I did everything right. My scrubs, even my mask, come off at the hospital, and I wash my hands thoroughly after taking them off. When I get home, I always take my street clothes off at the door and put them in a bag to be washed before changing into clean clothes. I've kept my distance from him, except for occasionally crossing

175

paths in the kitchen or on the way to the bathroom. That part was easy, because we had been staying in separate rooms ever since our agreement to divorce.

Yet here we are. Both with COVID. I was right that it was just a matter of time. Was it because thoughts become reality, or would it have happened no matter what? What exactly triggered it? I know I'm surrounded by it constantly, but I can't help but wonder. Did particles simply get through my mask and shield because their protection is not totally failproof? Was it from touching an infected surface and then touching my face? I try my best never to do that.

Could it have been from when I was holding Evelyn's hand? I flash back to that moment. I didn't realize it then, but I remember it now. I touched my mouth and my eyes when I wiped tears from them as she came back to life. I bet that was it. I may have helped save her life, but now my husband is sick because of it. Without trying to, I convince myself that's what happened. I really hope I don't have to take him to the hospital, but I reassure myself, if he does have to go, he's strong enough and young enough that he won't be there for long, that he will fight this, overcome his symptoms and be back home, back to normal, sooner rather than later.

It's been a week, and he's no better. I still can't believe it. I've done all I can. For him and for me, I think it's time to take him in so that he can get the care he needs. I simply don't have all the tools I need to care for him here. I've barely slept three hours a night, and I don't know how I've not gotten sick from exhaustion. I think all that pretending to be strong might be finally catching up to me. I enter the guest bedroom cautiously to see if Shane is asleep. His eyes are half-shut, but he opens them the best he can and looks at me with such a sad, desperate face.

"How are you feeling?" I say softly.

"I think you should take me to the hospital," he coughs.

A little bit of relief hits me because I thought for sure I'd have to convince him to go.

"OK. Do you want to go now?"

"When do you go to work?" he asks, confused.

"I can't work till I test negative twice," I tell him.

"Oh."

"I can take you, though. I'm not sick. Do you want me to help you get dressed?"

"Please," is all he manages to say, and then he closes his eyes briefly before opening them again.

"OK. Are your clothes in here or the closet?" I say, turning to the dresser.

"They're in there."

"Got it." I begin to open the top drawer and see, right on top, my favorite shirt of his. I think briefly about how much it meant to me for so long and how little it means now. I leave that shirt in the drawer and choose a different one. I don't want to be reminded of everything that was lost. I open the next drawer and pull out a pair of gym shorts. Then I find some socks, and I turn back to him. The situation feels very awkward, but I help him sit up and then help him get dressed. I try to treat him like any other patient I've ever helped get dressed or undressed. It works for the most part, as I'm able to push the thoughts of all we've been through out of my head. That's not what matters now. What matters is getting him to the hospital so he can get better.

———

He falls asleep on the way. I say his name to wake him up when we have arrived. He's so weak and fragile I have to help him walk in. I lead him to a chair and sit him down. The nurse at the front desk is obviously shocked to see me because I'm not supposed to be there, but she's more shocked to see Shane. I get him checked in and then leave immediately because of my positive test.

Worry engulfs me as I drive home. A part of me didn't want to take him because now I won't be able to take care of him. I know the doctors and nurses at the hospital are better equipped to do that, but a part of me wanted him to stay home so I could be the one to help him. It's a weird feeling because I know I don't love him anymore and that our marriage will still end when this

COVID thing is all over. So why do I feel the way I do?

I guess the nurturing part of my love never stopped. Maybe that's just who I am at my core. That's why I chose nursing as a career in the first place. Because I want to nurture and be there for people at their lowest. Wow! That hits me hard—like a revelation. I never looked at it that way before. Sure, not wanting to be around kids anymore was part of the reason I switched to the ICU, but helping the sick is just as big a part of it. I was blinded by the negative side for so long I couldn't see the other reason.

———

During the next couple of days, I call in every few hours to check on Shane. I usually call Beth or one of the other nurses.

"He's worse," Beth says.

"How's that possible? He's supposed to be getting better now," I say, feeling utterly confused.

She's not able to tell me much else before she has to let me go because someone needs her.

I'm still testing positive. I need to be there for him. He should be getting better now, not worse. Why did I wait so long to take him? I mean he was sick, but I've seen him almost that sick before, and he never had to go to the hospital. It was only because it was COVID and it's new, and we don't know all that much about it that I thought it would be a good idea. But he suggested going to the hospital before I could even tell him what I was thinking.

He must have been sicker than he was letting on. I guess he was just trying to power through it like he always did, but once he realized he wasn't getting better, he knew I should take him. Now he's stuck there, and I know they are taking good care of him the best they can, but nobody is getting the proper care they need because there are too many patients and not enough doctors and nurses. One less because I can't be there. It's so hard!

"Be strong," I hear my mother's voice in my head. "I'm trying, Mom," I say out loud as I turn on the water to the bathtub. I haven't taken a bath in ages, but I have to do something to try to calm my nerves. I may no longer love Shane, but I still care about him deeply and still want him to have the best life he possibly can. And that starts with him getting better, not worse.

———

The next day when I call, I can't believe the words I'm hearing.

"We had to put him on a ventilator," Beth says.

"What? You what? A ventilator?" I say in compete shock. "Is he going to make it?"

"I don't know, Amber. It's . . . It's not looking good. I'm sorry."

"No, he has to make it. He has to be a father someday," I say. I'm not sure why I added the father part, but I'm feeling hysterical right now and that's probably why. It's just what crossed my mind. I know it won't be with me, but that doesn't matter. He has to live. He's going to make a great husband for somebody and be a great dad. It just won't be me. But it has to be someone.

He can't die.

Amber

They are calling us heroes, those of us on the front lines, but if I were a hero, I would have found a way to save him. I'm anything but. It's my fault he's dead. I couldn't save him. He had no underlying issues, yet he is gone. Shane is dead. I don't understand.

It's my fault. I'm the reason he died. I feel so lost. Guilt consumes me. I should have been more careful. I should have been more conscious about touching my face. Why did I keep coming home to him after working around so many people with COVID? There had to have been another way. I could have . . . I could have . . . I don't know, but surely there was something I could have done differently, but it didn't happen. He's dead. I killed Shane. It's all my fault. How could I feel nothing and yet get him sick? It doesn't make any sense. Why does the virus show little or no symptoms for some people while it's a death sentence for others? I didn't even know I had COVID until I tested positive.

I don't understand any of it. I just know I'm the reason he's dead. His family will blame me, and they should. I don't want to ever set foot in another hospital again. I can't. I can't do it. What other choice do I

have, though? It's all I've ever done. It's not

like there are many places hiring right now.

The whole country is shut down. Even if it

wasn't, I don't feel like doing anything

anymore.

It's been a week. The shock has

worn off a little, but the pain and guilt are

the same. Shane's family told me they didn't

blame me, that there was no way to know

that the virus would kill him, but I don't

believe them. I know I'm the reason he's no

longer alive. Shane once told me that he

wanted to be cremated, and his mother was

OK with it. I can't believe I've caused so

much pain to so many people. It hurts so

bad. I cry and cry for hours until I'm so tired from crying that my body forces me to take a break. We will have to wait till life returns to normal before having a ceremony for him. I can't even imagine doing that. I don't see how people get through funerals soon after their loved ones die. I don't want to see or be around anyone right now. That's like the only silver lining in COVID; if you want to be alone, it is easy to do.

I hadn't tested myself again till just today, and I'm no longer testing positive. I'm told I can have another two weeks off but that they hope I can somehow bring myself to go back to work after that because of how much I'm needed. The hospital is paying for me to see a therapist via video

conference.

The therapist tells me it's not my

fault, but I still have a hard time shaking that

guilt. I don't think the sessions are helping.

Maybe if we could meet in person, I would

get more out of the sessions. There's only so

much that can be done in a video

conference. It's just not the same. It's not

personal. Her words barely penetrate the

surface of my tablet, of my problems. They

are dull as they come through the speakers. I

need to be there with her. My mental health

is shaky, and I know I'm not the only one

who feels this way right now.

I worry this virus is doing just as much damage to the mental health of people as it is physically. We can only be away from human connection for so long without losing it. We need hugs. We need to be there for each other. We need to do things together, *be* together. It's important. As much as I think I don't want to be around anybody right now, I know that I do need someone. I still know that we need each other. Wanting people to be back around each other while this is still going on is a hard thing for me to say as a nurse because I've seen the physical results of COVID so much and because of what I have done, but I've also seen in my patients' eyes that their spirits are crushed. I'm so confused by all my feelings; it's overwhelming.

———

It's been two weeks now. I'm still in no shape to return to work. I haven't worn anything but my pajamas since it happened. I'm running out of food, but getting dressed and going out somewhere seems like an impossible task. I'm lying here in bed, and it's time for another therapy session. I click on the video therapy, and as always, my therapist's smiling face greets me. Her name is Jennifer.

"Hi, Amber. How are you feeling?"

"A little better, I think," I say, trying to process.

"What has been on your mind lately?"

"I'm still fighting feelings that Shane's death is my fault."

"Are they still the same exact feelings? Or have they shifted at all?"

"The same, I think," I say, unsure of my answer.

"OK. Those feelings are based on an assumption that you know for sure you caused Shane to catch COVID, when in reality there is no way to know for sure exactly how Shane contracted the virus."

"I know, but I can't help it. It had to be from me."

"But you said he had been around other people as well."

"Not many."

"But it is still a possibility he caught the virus from someone else. There is no way of knowing with certainty, so you will never know. But if you are able to move past the assumption that you caused his death, you will begin to heal. When we assume, we pick up the paint brush to create a mental picture of a reality that may or may not be true. What do you think you can do to put down the paint brush?"

"I-I don't know. It just keeps replaying in my head over and over."

"Tell me again what Shane would want you to do."

"He would tell me to move on. He would tell me he wants me to eventually meet someone else and be happy, since we were going to get a divorce anyway. He would tell me it's not my fault."

"And do you believe that?"

"I'm trying."

"You didn't kill him. There were other factors playing a part, as well, as we've discussed previously," Jennifer says. "We can't control a tiny little thing that we cannot see."

"I know."

"What else would he tell you?"

"He would tell me to go back to work and try to keep helping people, but I can't. I can barely get out of bed. I can barely think of anything else but me getting him sick."

"Amber, this may seem like I'm telling you to do something that I have told you not to do, but I'm asking you to try something. Rather than assuming Shane's death was your fault, try to assume that it *wasn't* your fault."

"You want me to assume that he got sick some other way?"

"Exactly, because it's totally possible."

"OK, I will try."

"Are you still doing your meditation exercises like we talked about?"

"No. I mean, every now and then. I'm sorry."

"It's OK. Don't be sorry. I only want you to do the exercises when you are ready to do them."

"I can do the meditation. I'll be more consistent," I say, trying to mean it. Trying to muster the will to do it.

"OK, great. As you are breathing in, I want you to say to yourself, 'It's not my fault. I will assume the best, not the worst.' I know none of this is the best, but if you can feel that it's not your fault, you can move past where you are and begin to actually grieve his loss rather than continue to blame yourself.

"You are a strong person, Amber. I've talked with you enough now that I see your strength so clearly. I know you can free yourself of this feeling of guilt. It's only a matter of time. You will never fully be the same, but the new you will be in the best possible form someday. You are strong."

I don't say anything for a minute. I start to cry. Jennifer doesn't say anything, either. I'm crying because she said I was strong. I've tried to believe that I am like

Mom in that way, but it's been hard for me to internalize. Hearing Jennifer tell me I'm strong resonates with me. It sparks something in me. *I am strong*, I begin to tell myself, and then I guess I say it aloud because Jennifer responds, "Yes, you are strong. You are strong."

"Thank you," I say through the tears. *It's not my fault. It's not my fault. I am strong.* I don't care how many times I have to tell myself that; I believe it now. It's crazy how everything else she said to me didn't get through to me, but those three words, *you are strong*, have rocked me to my core. Even when I start to doubt it, I will keep telling myself, *It's not my fault; I am strong,* over and over until it's my new

reality.

Chase

Mom's stance on COVID has drastically changed since she almost died. She's more cautious, and oddly enough, I've gone a bit the other way. I think I have grown less anxious about it because they are saying that once you've had COVID, you have enough antibodies to resist the virus for a while. Her doctor says it's OK for us to be around each other, at least for now. Summer is almost here, and with the warmer weather, the numbers are starting to go down, which helps ease my fear as well. When fall and winter come, we may have to go back to being away from each other, but for now we are living life normally for the most part—as normal as can be in such an unprecedented time.

Still, I try not to hug her, but every so often she will give me a hug before she goes to bed, and it's always very brief. We both agree to stay out of each other's face as best we can, but now we do watch movies together—her in the recliner and me on the couch. We eat at the table, too, with her at one end and me at the other. The newspaper provides a little protection, as well, I guess, because I can't even see her face at times. She shakes her head when she reads more about what happened last week, about

George Floyd and everything that's resulting from it. The whole country has gone mad.

"It's such a horrible thing, but I don't think burning down our cities is the answer," she says to me.

"It's crazy. It's all crazy," I say. "First COVID, now this. We are definitely not going to forget 2020. That's for sure."

Neither of us says anything as she continues to read the rest of the article. Then she flips the page.

"Oh, wow! That's her," Mom says, throwing the rest of the paper to the side and keeping only the page she's reading.

"Who is it?" I ask curiously.

"Oh, my gosh," she says, so lost in what she's reading that she fails to realize I have said anything.

"What is it, Mom?"

"Oh, that poor girl."

I drop my spoon into my cereal bowl, stand up, and walk behind Mom so I can see what all the fuss is about.

There's a picture of a nurse, and she's being handed some kind of award for her work on the front line. I see the headline:

'Widowed nurse honored for her bravery'

"That's Amber," Mom says, sniffling.

"Who's Amber?"

"That's the nurse who saved my life."

"Really?"

"Yes. I had no idea her husband died. That's so sad," Mom says, running her finger across the picture of Amber.

"That's terrible. She saves you, and then her husband dies. Oh, man. I feel so bad for her," I say. It really hits me. My mom wouldn't be here if it wasn't for her. She didn't deserve to lose her husband. She is a hero. Heroes don't deserve that. I don't even know her, but her loss strikes me as if I do. Mom and I sit in silence for a moment, staring at her picture.

"She's pretty, isn't she?"

"She's very pretty," I say. "Didn't you write her a thank-you letter?"

"Yes. The hospital gave it to her, and she even wrote me back saying she was glad I made it and how I reminded her of her own mother. I even mailed her a present, remember? But I never heard back from her after that. I was surprised she didn't get back to me, but it makes sense now with her husband dying. I just can't believe it. I need to reach out to her again."

She doesn't wait. She calls the hospital immediately, and I'm surprised when they are able to get Amber on the phone. Mom has a habit of putting her phone calls on speaker, so I'm able to hear the entire conversation.

"Amber, this is Evelyn. I'm so sorry about your husband. I just saw it in the paper. Is there anything I can do for you?"

"Hi, Evelyn. Thank you. That's really sweet. I'm OK. I mean I'm so *not* OK, but I'm gonna make it. I am strong. I appreciate you calling," Amber says, her voice that of an angel who has come crashing down from heaven with a broken wing.

"I wish there was something I could do for you," Mom says hopelessly.

"It's OK. Really. Thank you so much," Amber says politely.

"If you need anything or anybody to talk to, you can call me anytime," Mom says, as if Amber were her own daughter. It reminds me of how Mom has always treated me when I'm feeling down.

"Thank you," Amber says softly.

"You're welcome. I'll let you get back to work. I'm sorry to call you while you're working."

"That's all right. I appreciate it." Amber pauses for a brief moment. "You were my favorite patient, you know. I'll never forget you. You are an absolute miracle," Amber says with complete reverence. Her kindness radiates through the phone.

"Oh, my gosh, you are so sweet. Did you get the gift I sent you?" Mom asks.

"You sent me a gift? No, I never got anything," Amber says, sounding puzzled.

"Really? I figured you were going through so much that you didn't think of reaching back out to me, which I totally understand."

"No, I would have. I never got it. I swear. What was it?"

"Well, I bought one for me, too, and I'll give you that one," I hear Mom say emphatically.

"You don't have to do that."

"It's no problem."

"Actually, how about I just bring it to you, so we don't take the chance of it getting lost in the mail again?"

"Well, that's really sweet but probably not the best idea," Amber says hesitantly.

"You're right, but we both have antibodies now. We should be fine," Mom says, her persistent nature beginning to kick in.

"I know. It's just that the hospital would kind of frown upon it."

"I could bring it by your house and give it to you outside, if that works. If it's not too much of a problem."

"Really, it's not a big deal. You don't have to give me anything."

"Or what if my son and I met you somewhere, like at a park or something?" Mom says.

"Well, I guess that would be OK. I could meet you at a park. That's fine. It would be really nice to see you again. I came back for my next shift, and you were already gone. I thought the worst when I didn't see you. I was in shock for a moment because I thought you'd taken a turn, and well—but then I asked, and they said you had already been discharged. It made me so happy."

"I'm so glad. So, you'll meet us then?" Mom asks.

"I can meet you at the park sometime, but we'll have to keep our distance."

"That's fine. I mean, I'd love to give you a big hug for everything you did for me, but I won't. Maybe someday."

"Maybe someday," Amber repeats.

"When are you off work again?"

"I have two more twelve-hour shifts the next two days, but then I'm off on Monday."

"Oh, you poor thing, having to work all those long hours."

"It's rough, but it's all I can do. I have to keep helping people," Amber says with sadness and passion.

Her words make me want to hug her too, to try and pull the sadness from her and to thank her for saving Mom.

"Monday afternoon around two, OK?"

"Sounds good," Amber says.

"Perfect!"

"I better get back to work. I'm so glad you called, though. I'll see you Monday."

"I look forward to it," Mom says.

And after all I heard during their conversation, I'm looking forward to it as well. I owe her everything.

Chase

A few days later, we are on our way to the park to meet Amber. I feel a few butterflies in my stomach as we get closer. I wonder if she's as nice in person as she sounded on the phone. I'm sure she will be. Why am I so anxious? I guess it's because we are in the middle of a pandemic, and we are about to go meet someone in public. That doesn't feel like the reason, though. I think it's because to me it's like I'm going to meet my hero. I have her to thank for my favorite person in the entire world still being here with me. If it wasn't for her, my life would be in shambles right now. Then I think again about how her life probably *does* feel like it is in shambles. That makes me feel bad for her again, and again I want to hug her, even though I know I can't.

As we turn into the park, I see her sitting on a bench up ahead in the distance waiting for us.

"That's her, isn't it?" I ask.

"That's her. I told you she was pretty," Mom says as we pull into a parking spot.

"Very," I say. She must have heard in my voice exactly what I was thinking. *She's not just pretty; she's beautiful.* Then it hits me. I'm nervous because I'm attracted to her. I try to push the thought away because of all that she has gone through, and then all sorts of different mixed emotions hit me. I want to hurry from the car to meet her, and at the same time, I want to turn around and leave the park.

I reach into the back seat to grab the small bag with Amber's present. We get out of the car and Amber stands up, waves to us, and smiles at Mom. We begin to walk her way, and with every step, I become more aware of my every movement, not wanting to look stupid. I'm really nervous. I can't help but be stunned by her beauty. Her long hair and slim, but not too slim, figure are exactly what I picture when I think about the woman of my dreams. There's more to her than just the way she looks, though. More than what's on the surface, and somehow I can sense it, even though she looks tired and depressed.

I immediately feel for her again and push away my other thoughts. I don't know her at all, but I want to go up to her and wrap my arms around her. I want to tell her everything is going to be all right. That's not possible, of course.

She is a mere ten feet from us when we stop. She starts to put on her mask, and I'm about to do the same.

"We won't come any closer, so you don't have to put your mask on. You are too beautiful to hide your face," Mom says. Amber stops and lets her mask hang over her ear. I stuff mine back into my pocket.

"Thanks. It's nice to see you, How are you?" Amber aks.

"Oh, my goodness. Is it ever! I'm good. So nice to see you again, too. I promise we will keep our distance. Air hug!" Mom says, reaching her arms out and putting her hands together.

I can't help but laugh at Mom's ridiculousness, and it helps ease my butterflies. Amber notices my laugh, and our eyes connect for a brief moment. She smirks at me like she knows exactly why I was laughing.

"Amber, this is my son, Chase," Mom says.

"Hi, Chase," she says with a smile. I can tell it's a little hard for her to smile through her pain, but somehow the smile is still so genuine. I nod awkwardly.

"Hi" is all I can say at first. I try to look directly at her, and she looks at me for only a second before looking down. "I'm so grateful you were there for her," I say, turning to glance at Mom.

"I was just doing my job," Amber says, looking up at me with the most honest and humble of responses.

I turn back toward her and say, "I'm sorry for your loss."

She looks down at the ground again. "It's OK," she tells me, but all I hear is pain in her voice, and I know that it's not. I can tell she wants to say more, but she doesn't. Amber looks back up but doesn't meet my eyes again. She looks at the bag in my hand.

"Here it is," Mom says, reaching out to take the gift from me.

"You didn't have to—"

"Open it," Mom says, handing it to her quickly and then stepping back just as fast.

Amber smiles as she takes the gift out of the bag. Her pain seems to disappear for a moment as she sees the Tim McGraw

CD. I see a few tears slip down her cheeks, but her smile says they're happy tears.

"Your voice was like magic to me," Mom says. "It brought me back to life." I can tell she's starting to get emotional. I'm able to maintain my composure for now.

"I-I didn't even realize you could hear me," Amber says.

"I did," Mom says, and there are tears on her face, too.

I turn away to fight back tears of my own.

"I'm guessing he's your favorite?" Mom says, referring to Tim McGraw.

"He is," Amber says, wiping tears from her face. "I've seen him in concert ten times."

I imagine myself being there with her at one of those concerts. I see myself dancing with her on the lawn at the amphitheater. We dance and sing each verse together, smiling and staring at each other the entire time. I snap out of it quickly so I don't appear aloof, and we continue to talk about music. I don't say much, though. I'm lost in the way she speaks, the way she carries herself. More butterflies course through my entire body when she looks my way. I try to fight them off. I shouldn't be having feelings like that at a time like this. I try to hide my emotions, but I don't know if it's working. I think she can tell. That makes me uneasy, and a part of me is ready to leave.

But the way she has been looking at me, looking directly at me but looking quickly away when I look directly at her, makes me wonder if she's feeling the same butterflies. Maybe I'm imagining it, but I feel as if there is a palpable energy, some sort of strange cosmic wave washing over us both right now. That makes me want to stay.

After another five minutes—the feeling never leaving or letting up for a single second—we begin to say our goodbyes, but I don't want to say goodbye.

227

When I do, it will likely be the last time I see her, and I can't live with that. What has come over me?

I remember Mom mentioned something about her and her husband planning to get a divorce before everything happened with COVID, but it's too weird. *He's dead. It's too soon. I can't. I have to. I can't. I'll look like a complete asshole. I have to.* My thoughts are jumbled, but something deep inside me is telling me to ask her if she'd like to take a walk sometime. In this same park would be fine. I will hate myself if I don't ask, but I might hate myself if I do. I'll never know what could be if I don't ask, though, and I can't live with that. The regret of never knowing because I didn't ask is more intense than the fear of looking completely stupid. Her beauty and kindness warm me, just like the sun, which is shining brightly. I try to stop myself, but the words leave my mouth before I realize it.

"Maybe we could meet here again sometime and take a walk, you and I," I say timidly. I have no idea how Mom is reacting to what I said because I'm too focused on Amber.

Amber hesitates as she gathers her thoughts. *What is she thinking?* I want to know. *What am I doing? That was so dumb. I have to take it back.* I'm about to tell her

"Never mind" and that I'm sorry for asking, but she speaks before I do.

"Um, sure," she says, like she wanted to say no, but she couldn't. Maybe the same thing that compelled me to ask her out compelled her to say yes. I feel it even more now, and I'm no longer doubting that she feels it, too. It truly is as if our energies are perfectly aligned. Because of everything going on with COVID and her being a nurse, I should have never asked, and she should have never said yes, but that's not what has happened. What is going to happen is we are going to go on a socially distanced walk through the park in the near future, the same path together, one step at a time.

Amber

I've come a long way in such a short period of time. I've broken through with Jennifer on my therapy calls, and we've gained so much traction since she called me "strong," and I fully embraced it. It's still hard, but I'm healing. I've healed so much that I even agreed to meet Chase to go on a walk with him here in the park. I'm sitting on the bench trying to talk myself into leaving, but I feel like I'm glued to this bench.

It's not something I thought I would be capable of doing again—meeting another man. Especially in the middle of a pandemic. There is something about him that wouldn't let me say no, though. I don't know what it is, but I'm willing to wait for him to get here to figure it out. I still haven't gotten over Shane dying, but I don't blame myself anymore. I knew we were going to get a divorce and that all our love was lost. But he was my husband and he's gone, and it sucks really bad. Jennifer has helped me come to accept that, though.

I'm still tired all the time, too, but that's OK. Right now, I'm exhausted from working back-to-back double shifts, and I should be sleeping. Instead, here I am, watching the tree limbs bend at the will of the wind. I worry that I might get too close to Chase and get him sick, too. Why am I willing to risk it? I don't understand it. I should be staying away from people more than anyone. My job is only going to get worse if this thing doesn't end, and I know it's wrong for me to be here. So why am I here?

I really should leave before he arrives. I could blame it on him being late, if only that were true. It's not. I'm fifteen minutes early. That's how excited I am to meet him. There's something about him. He's different than any man I've ever met in my entire life. But how would I really know? I barely talked to him when his mom came to give me the CD. Is it simply the way he looked at me? Did he feel it, too? This strange magnetic pull, as if we are being drawn toward each other. He must have felt it. If he hadn't, he would not have been so bold as to ask a nurse out on a date in the middle of a pandemic. I never saw that coming. He seemed so shy, but it was so cute. And then after being so reserved, he asked to meet me again. I was blown away.

I'm not leaving, even if he does end up being late. I'm going to sit right here and wait for him. I want to know all about him. Who he is. Where he came from. What kind of man he is. Why I like him so much.

He arrives right on time. Not a minute early, not a minute late. I stand as he stops a few steps before he reaches me.

"Hellooo," he says with a goofy smile, and I can tell right away he's comfortable being himself around me before we even start walking. He was so nervous when he asked to meet me, yet so quirky now. I like quirky. I'm even more attracted to him. I'm so caught up in my thoughts that I forget to say hi. I'm just standing here smiling at him like a weirdo, but it doesn't bother him.

"Shall we?" he says.

"Oh, yes. Hi, Chase. We shall," I say, and immediately I feel stupid.

With each step down the path, I feel more and more comfortable. Neither of us mentions the pandemic at first. Thank God. It's a relief. Instead, we make small talk about the park, and then we talk about meeting here for the first time.

"Your mom is the absolute best," I tell him. It really made my—" I hesitate. It definitely made more than my day. "It made my whole month," I say. "In fact, it's probably the best thing that's happened to me since this whole thing started. I'm so happy she survived. I don't know if it really was my singing or not, but I'm so thankful she's still here for you, Chase." I try not to tear up. I can sense he's starting to feel the weight of my words, too.

"Thank you, Amber. I-I don't know what I'd do without her." He takes a deep breath, as if to calm his emotions.

"So have you picked up any crazy indoor hobbies since we can't go anywhere or do anything?" I ask him before we both start crying.

"Um, sort of. It's kind of embarrassing, though." He smiles and lets out a short, nervous chuckle.

"What is it?" I begin to laugh. "I won't make fun of you, I promise," I tell him, and I mean it.

"Well, if you promise, then OK," he says, and stops.

"And?" I draw the word out in anticipation.

"I've gotten back into trading cards."

"Trading cards? Like Pokémon or something?"

"No, almost as bad, though. Sports cards. I've gone through all my old ones that I had from a long time ago, and I've even been buying some online, even though I've only gotten one box so far because of shipping delays."

"That's cool. So, like just baseball cards or basketball, too?" I ask him, not bothered at all by it.

"Baseball, basketball, football, hockey—you name it. I feel like a kid again; I'm not going to lie. And honestly, it's felt pretty darn good. It's like I gained my innocence back or something."

"Wow. Very interesting. Any of them worth any money?"

"No, no, not really," he laughs.

"Darn."

"Well, actually I did find one last night that's worth a couple hundred, it looks like."

"What is it?"

"It's an old Hulk Hogan card."

"Wrestling, huh?"

"Yep. My guilty pleasure. I've always been a fan. Can't help it," he says, shrugging his shoulders.

"Oh, really?"

"You're probably ready to leave now, huh?"

"Hmm." I stop walking and pretend I'm thinking about leaving, even though I'm hoping he can tell I'm joking because I'm about to start giggling. "Well, if I left, then I'd have to say, 'You can't see me!'" I wave my hand in front of my face and laugh.

"John Cena? Really! Are you a closet wrestling fan, too?" He looks like he's in complete shock. The smile on his face is so adorable.

"Fully out of the closet when it comes to wrestling. Almost everyone rolls their eyes when I try to tell them about it."

"You're kidding, right?"

"Nope!" I say, staring right at him. It's much easier to look at him now than it was when we first met. All our silly teenager-like tension is gone.

He's elated. Both of just look at each other and laugh for what feels like a lifetime. I needed this so bad—all my worries may as well be five hundred miles away right now. I can't believe it. Turns out we are both a couple of wrestling nerds.

"How did you get into it?" he asks me.

"Well, I used to go over to my grandma and grandpa's house as a kid every Saturday. All day long. My parents would drop me off and then pick up me Sunday morning. That was their night out after a long week. But anyway, we were all sitting in the living room one night after dinner, Grandpa clicking through the channels rapidly like he always does until he finds something he likes, and I noticed something. 'Go back, Grandpa,' I told him. But he clicks too far onto some movie. 'Nope, one more up. Look! Look! That guy looks like you, Grandpa!' We proceeded to watch the rest of the match, and I was mesmerized by it. At first I thought it was just because the wrestler looked like Grandpa, but it turns out I was in love with wrestling from the moment I saw it."

"Who was it?"

"Arn Anderson. *WCW Saturday Night.*"

"Oh, wow! Classic. That's great."

"Thank God for Grandpa, right?"

"Indeed!"

"What about you? How'd you fall in love with it?" I ask him.

"You know, honestly, sad to say, but I don't really remember. Guess I was clicking through the channels, and it just caught my eye, too."

We talk wrestling for quite a while longer and discuss who our favorites are and what shows we've been to.

"I'm shocked. I can't believe we both like wrestling. Maybe we can go to a show together if and when they ever start having them again," he says, and we start to walk again.

"That would be fun," I say, thinking of what shirt I'd wear to the show and how it would go. I wonder if we both would root for the same wrestler every match or if one of us would go for the other and think how fun it would be if that happened.

Neither of us says anything for a minute or so. We take in our surroundings once more, and I think about everything we've said so far. It gets harder to maintain a six-foot distance the farther we walk. I want to blame it on the sidewalk being too small, but that's not it at all. I feel like we are two magnets being drawn together with each step we take.

I don't want to keep a distance. I want to get close to him. I wish he'd reach out and hold my hand. I'm sure he would have done it already in normal times. I want to stop at the clearing up ahead and sit on the bench with him. Right next to me, our legs touching, our hands intertwined. It goes against everything that's happening in this world right now, but I feel like it's bound to happen. We are at the bench now.

"Wanna stop and sit down?" he asks, as if he's read my mind. "I'll sit at one end, and you can sit at the other," he says before I can answer.

"Sure, that works," I say. Before we know it, hours have passed and the sun is setting.

"I know this is so, so stupid," he says. "But it's taken everything in me to keep my distance from you, and I was wondering—" He stops. "Ahh, never mind. Never mind."

"You want to kiss me?" I ask, but before he answers, something comes over me, and I leap into his arms and kiss him deeply. He tastes so sweet, like everything I've ever wanted. I don't care about COVID at all right now. When we stop kissing after a minute or so, he looks deeply into my eyes for a second and then begins to laugh softly.

"What?" I giggle.

"I was only going to ask you for a hug," he smirks.

"Oh," I say, shrugging my shoulders.

He walks me back to my car, and like a gentleman opens my door, gives me a quick peck on the lips, and shuts my car door for me after I'm in. He begins to walk away but is still turned partially towards me as he does, and we both wave. By the look on his face, I can tell he doesn't regret any of it, and neither do I.

Amber

We've been on four dates in the past four weeks, but it feels like I've known him forever. We've gone to the same park each time and made out in the woods like a couple of teenagers when no one was around to see us. Even if there were people watching, they wouldn't know that we'd just recently met. They would think we had been together since before the pandemic, and therefore, being in close contact wouldn't be inappropriate. Or would it?

There are other nurses at work who don't even sleep in the same room as their husbands. I mean, I tried not to be around Shane when he was still alive, but that was not only because of the pandemic. It was because we were going to separate. And there are other nurses with boyfriends they don't live with, and they've chosen not to see them until the numbers go down more.

I feel like I'm doing something wrong by seeing Chase, but it feels so right. It feels like what I've been waiting for my entire life. We get along fabulously. We haven't disagreed on anything—not one single thing. It's too perfect. *He's* too perfect. It's got to be too good to be true, doesn't it? I try over and over again to find something wrong, to stop this foolishness of dating someone new in the middle of a pandemic. If my supervisor at the hospital found out about it, I wonder if I could get fired. I don't see how, but nothing would surprise me anymore. It would certainly be frowned upon. I'd be the black sheep of the nursing community. So be it. In many ways, I feel like I already am.

I'm sitting on the same bench waiting for him, just like the first day we met. We could meet somewhere else, I suppose, but neither of us has suggested it. I don't think we care. As long as we are together, it doesn't matter. I want so badly to invite him back to my place after our walk this evening. What would it matter if we got even closer—if we were intimate? We are already in close contact for extended periods of time.

Here he comes. I'm grinning from ear to ear. At first we don't talk about COVID, but inevitably it comes up. We talk about his mom.

"Are you still staying away from her, then? Chase, I hate that you have to do that, and if you tell me you don't want to see me anymore, I will understand."

"She's all right with it. Really, she is. She's definitely more protective about COVID since she almost died, but she knows how much I like you, and she wants us to be together. Plus, she thinks since she's had it so bad already, she won't be able to get it again. At least not for a while."

"She's probably right, but no one knows for sure. Even with you guys staying apart, though, what if she still gets it? I thought I was careful around Shane, but he still got it, and look what happened. I can't have that happen again with your mom, or with you. I won't be the reason someone dies again. It's my job to *save* people from dying of COVID, not kill them because I'm careless."

"It's her choice. I told her all this, and she knows. She accepts the risk and so do I. It's on her, not you."

"But I still have a choice, and if I choose to keep my distance from you for a while then there would be no risk, but—"

"But?"

"But I don't want to, Chase. I want to get even closer to you. I want—" I hesitate.

"I want it, too. I want you to come back to the house with me. I want you to stay with me, but obviously that would never work." He frowns.

"No, it won't. But I know something that would."

"You want me to stay with you?"

"I do. Very badly. I want you to make love to me before we go to sleep and then again when we wake. We could go back to sleep after or just lie there and cuddle as long as possible until it's time for me to go to work."

"I'd absolutely love that," he says with a radiant smile.

"But then how would you be able to take care of your mom? You can't leave her."

"She lived without me for several years. I know she would be fine. I could still be there for her. I'll ask her how she feels about it."

"It would actually keep her safer because then you could visit her and stay outside and never get close."

"I think it could work. It would be the best of both worlds. I could be with you more and also keep her safe."

"Only if she's one hundred percent OK with it."

"She likes you a lot. I have a feeling she's going to think it's a great idea."

He's right. She *will* think it's a great idea. She likes me so much, and I'm pretty sure she can tell that I'm in love with her son.

Amber

It's late summer now. The flowers and trees are full of life, and so is our love. I'm as happy as I can remember being. The thought of getting him or his mother sick still rattles around in the back of my head, but I don't worry about it nearly as much because the COVID numbers continue to decline. Work is still brutal, but knowing I'm coming home to him makes it all worth it.

Mondays are the best. My only day off. We sleep in late, then we go to the park where we first met for a walk. From the park, we go to an early dinner at one of the select places that have reopened for distanced dine-in. We go early to make sure we are home in time to watch WWE's *Monday Night Raw*.

It's weird watching it without a crowd there, but we cheer and boo in an exaggerated way to make up for the absence. *Raw* cuts to commercial. Chase touches my arm, then begins to rub my leg. An unexplainable energy shoots through me. It happens every time we touch. I lean into him and rub my head on his shoulder. When I look up, he stares deeply into my eyes and kisses me gently. He pauses and pulls away just enough to look into my eyes again. The next kiss is longer and with more intensity. We make out passionately, and I work my hand down his chest. We both pull away, though, at the roar of the crowd as *Raw* comes back from commercial. Was the entire pandemic merely a nightmare that somehow miraculously turned into the happiest dream I've ever had? Was I about to wake up? It's only a second before we realize they are showing highlights from a match that happened before COVID ever hit. In the middle of the replay, the camera cuts away to a young kid in the crowd jumping up and down, cheering as "the face"—the good guy—gets the three-count on the bad guy, "the heel." The kid was so excited that as he jumped up, he knocked the popcorn out of his dad's hand, and it went everywhere.

Chase laughs, but my heart sinks, and I'm overcome with a sudden urge to tell him the only thing I've ever hidden from him. I said I'd never lie about it again, but I've kept it from him. It almost came up once before, but I was thankful it didn't. I'm not OK with it anymore. I've been dreading this moment, but I knew it was inevitable. I can't live with this fear anymore, and I owe it to him to tell him. I love him too much. For better or for worse, now is the time. I don't know where this is coming from, but the pull is too strong to ignore.

"Are you OK?" he says, sensing my change in emotion.

"No, Chase. It's the kid."

"The kid who spilled the popcorn?"

"Yes," I say, tears beginning to form.

"What about him?" he asks.

"I . . . I can't have any." Tears pour from my eyes. "I . . . I can't have kids."

He doesn't say anything, and the look on his face barely changes. "Oh—"

I cut him off in fear of what he might say. "I'm so sorry. I should have told you sooner. I told myself I would be upfront about it if I ever started dating again, but I hid it from you anyway. I'm sorry. I should have come clean before, but I was afraid you would leave me. I'm so sorry. If you want to have kids and you don't want to be with me anymore, I would be devastated, but I would understand. I would. I don't want to ever be the reason someone isn't able to see their dreams come true, to raise a family. I won't—"

"Amber. Amber. Stop, baby. Listen to me. It's OK," he says, gently touching my face to wipe each tear away one by one.

"It is?" I say as the fear begins to leave me.

"Yeah, it's perfectly fine," he says, then kisses my forehead.

"Are you sure?"

"Yes. It's OK," he says, kissing my forehead again for reassurance. "I promise."

"You don't want to have any? You don't want a family?"

"I want to have *you*. That's what I want," he says, moving his hands from my face to my hips.

"But you're OK if we never have any kids? Completely OK with it?" I say to erase all doubts.

"Yes, sweetheart. Sure, at one point in my life, I thought like everyone else. I thought having kids is what you were supposed to do. But after a while, I realized not everyone does, and if I was one of the ones who didn't, I was completely fine with that. Besides, we can still have a family if we want one. There are still ways."

"I've tried all the ways, Chase. Shane and I explored every option we had—medicines, IUI, IVF, you name it—but I just can't conceive. The doctors say it's impossible."

"Maybe so. I'm not talking about that, though. I'm talking about adoption."

Michael

I can't believe it, but I've been here for a year now. Mom pleaded guilty. She was sentenced to thirty years in prison. I'll be old by the time she gets out, if she's even still alive. It sucks. I'd like to see her again, but they don't think I'm ready. I'm not sure I am either so I don't push it. When I am ready, though, I will visit her and thank her for sacrificing her freedom to give me mine.

Life in general still kind of sucks, but at least things are getting somewhat back to normal. We were able to take off the masks briefly during the summer and fall, but once it started getting colder again and the number of cases started rising once more, they made us put them back on again until spring. They are off again now and hopefully for good because I promised myself I would never wear one again. It's ridiculous at this point. It's been over a year. I still see people wearing them sometimes, and it blows my mind.

I'm saying this right now because my CPS caseworker, Ms. Myra, still wears one all the freaking time. She's called me in here to her office for God-only-knows-what, and I won't be able to understand half of what she says because it will be muffled through that stupid mask. I think she says something about being held up by one of the

kids as she enters the room, but I don't hear

why. I barely even turn around. She begins

to sit down, and I'm shocked when she takes

off her mask. I sit up in my seat because I

know what she's going to tell me must be

important. She smiles. Could it be? Does

someone actually want to adopt me? Her

smile gets bigger, and then she tells me the

good news.

———

They will be here any moment. The

anticipation is killing me. What will they be

like? Will they be crazy like my biological

parents were, each in their own way? Or maybe, just maybe, they will be normal. I asked my foster mom why they picked me; how come they didn't want someone younger? She didn't have any real answers, though—only that they wanted someone a little older because they didn't want to start from scratch. I bet it's because they didn't want to have to deal with all the problems that come with babies and then toddlers. That makes me like them more because I wouldn't want to deal with it, either.

Having to be around little kids all the time like I've been doing this past year has been rough. I mean, it's not all bad; it's just a lot sometimes. I'm ready to be an only child again. Parents who love me are all I need.

Doubt creeps in. What if they meet me and then change their minds? Why did they agree to adopt me before ever having met me? Is it because they read my file and they feel sorry for me? Ms. Myra says it's a trial run and to be good so that they will want to keep me. "Temp to perm," she says. I can't think about the possible temporary part, though. I have to believe I've found my forever home. I will do everything I can to make them like me. As long as they are good to me, I will be good to them. I don't want to die anymore. I want to finish growing up with them as my parents. I want to live a long life and be happy.

Ms. Myra's phone buzzes, and she looks down briefly before putting her mask back on. "They're here," she says. "I'll be right back." She's probably gone no more than a couple of minutes, but it feels like hours. Finally, I see shadows in the hall, and I can hear her talking to them. I can't make out what she's saying, though. I think she asked them something. I hear the man say "No." NO? Do they not want me anymore? What happened? Are they going to leave?

Familiar old thoughts enter my mind, and the past comes at me like a wave. It's my fault. No one loves me. What is wrong with me? I want to run, but they are all out there in the hallway, and I have no other way to escape. I rip off my mask so I can breathe better. I take a long, deep breath, and as I do, Ms. Myra comes back into the room. I see the man and the woman right behind her. I watch as they toss their masks into the trash can. That's why he said "No!" He didn't want to wear the mask, and neither did she. The past evaporates as quickly as it comes, and a newfound hope rises with the smiles on their faces. I stand up, and I can't help but smile, too.

"Hi, Michael. I'm Chase," the man says, reaching out his hand.

"And I'm Amber," the woman says, her face beaming with pure joy.

I'm fighting back tears because I can feel it in the core of my soul. They will be good to me. I know it as though it's something I've *always* known. Like our lives were meant to cross in the middle of these crazy times. Maybe there is a God after all. I know in my heart it will not be temporary. "I'm Michael," I say, and without thinking, I lunge into their arms, and we all cry. At last, I have a complete, loving family.

-The End-

Acknowledgements

I'd like to thank my dad for saying I should document those crazy times while they were happening in the form of a story, that turned into this novella. Thanks to Darcy for being my beta reader, my development editor Michael, copy editor Allison, and my proofreader Lori. All of you did a fantastic job. Thank you, Linda, for helping me with my cover. That was a fun day. I hope that's everybody. If I missed anyone, please don't take my lack of memory personally. God bless.

COMING SOON

The Bottom Drops Out

Please enjoy a preview in the following

pages.

Prologue

Late 2000

Baseball was the furthest thing from Jake Matthews's mind that night. How does the old saying go? You can choose your friends—which he had done poorly—but you can't choose your family, and his was dysfunctional to be sure. He'd been a highly sought-after high school prospect, but by the time he got to college he was half gone, his fastball dead, his changeup departed, his curveball flatlined.

275

"In, out, up, down. He just

can't seem to find command

of the strike zone . . . "

It was well after eleven p.m. when a vacant-eyed, meager man named Tony, wearing a Cardinals hat cocked sideways and a ratty gray coat and jeans, approached him in a patch of trees down by the Gateway Arch. Normally, Jake sold only to other students and teammates who were trying to get their fix. Tonight was different though, his buyer different. Jake had met Tony only a few hours before.

Shuffling through the leaves, Tony made his way to Jake, who was waiting on the path, and stopped a little too close for comfort. Jake casually took a step back, hoping Tony wouldn't notice, but he did.

"Relax, man! We're all friends here. You got the goods?"

"Yes, I've got—" Jake paused midsentence as a jogger came into view. The woman approached slowly at first but started running faster as she neared the shady situation. For a split-second Jake and Tony were on the same page, admiring tight yoga pants and long brown hair flopping in a ponytail as she whizzed by. She faded into the distance, and it was back to business.

"Well, let's see it," Tony said.

Jake reached into his jacket pocket and pulled out a glassine bag containing four small rocks.

"You wantin' sixty bucks for it, right?" Tony asked.

"No, man, it's eighty bucks like I said on the phone, sorry, or twenty dollars a rock. However many you want."

"Come on! Cut me a deal here."

"I can't, man, then I wouldn't be making any money. You understand," Jake said, not realizing he'd just poked the bear.

Tony was offended. "You think I'm dumb? I understand just fine. You don't need that extra money. Your mama and papa prolly hand you all kinds of money."

Jake had no idea the snake was about to strike.

"Tonight's pitching matchup features Jake Matthews, a six-foot-four, two-hundred-twenty-pound righty from Saint Louis. This kid is strong and talented but has a few character issues that need ironing out. And he will be opposed by Tony Owens, a five-foot-nine, one-hundred and-sixty-five-pound soft-tossing lefty, a junkballer

trying to hold on as long as

possible. It certainly looks

like a mismatch on

paper . . ."

"Look! I'm sorry, man. I can't do it. I'll

sell you three of them for fifty bucks. That's

the—"

Before Jake could say another word,

Tony reached into his coat pocket.

Oh, shit! He's got a gun, Jake thought.

"And the runner dives

headfirst into second base.

What's the call? And he

is . . ."

Jake dove toward Tony, trying to grab his arm. The crack bag went flying as Jake crashed to the ground. Instead of a gun, out came a switchblade. Jake stumbled to his knees and Tony pounced on top of him, burying the metal deep in Jake's side. Once, then twice. Tony grabbed the crack bag and was gone.

Jake pressed his hands to his side. Blood gushed from his body and began to pool between his lips. The knife had hit a vital organ—his lung—which was filling up with blood. He was suffocating and bleeding out at the same time. Thoughts and memories flooded his brain at warp speed as time seemed to stretch exponentially. He dug deep for the tiny sliver of energy he had left and let out a desperate plea.

"Help! Help! Help! I've been—" Jake tried shouting, but he was barely able to breathe. All he could do was gasp. His voice grew faint. "Help, I've been stabbed."

His volume dropped further with each passing second. Maybe someone would come by. Maybe the midnight jogger would hear him. His eyes moved from side to side searching for her, for anyone. His consciousness was quickly fading—death was on its way—set in motion, long before that night.

*****If you enjoyed the book, please kindly leave a review.
They play a cruical role in the book's success. Thank you.*****

How to leave a review

1.   Go to your Amazon Account and find my book or go to
garymartinbooks.com and click on the proper book (BELOW IS
ONLY AN EXAMPLE).

2.   Scroll down to where it says **review this product** and click on
write a customer review or click on the stars where the book has
already been rated, click see all reviews, then click on write a
customer review.

3.   Rate the book and leave your review.

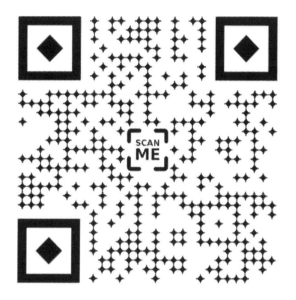

garymartinmedia.com

Thank you for reading. For more books and

my other projects please check out

https://www.garymartinmedia.com

About the author

Gary is from Southern Illinois and has a passion for sports and philosophy. He earned his bachelor's degree in Journalism and spent 11 years in radio sportscasting, garnering many awards, including best play-by-play broadcaster for the state of Illinois. After accomplishing his goals in broadcasting, he left that career to pursue his passion for writing. He is in the process of publishing his debut novel, The Bottom Drops Out, and his poetry book, Sanity In The Chaos. His Novella Distant Times and his short story series Dreamland are

available now.

Made in the USA
Columbia, SC
20 March 2025

55455768R00174